the MEADOW and the MISREAD

the Meadow and the Misread

Max Halper

Threadsuns 2022
High Point, NC

Published by Threadsuns, High Point, NC 27268

First Edition
25 24 23 22 21 5 4 3 2 1

ISBN 978-1-7346911-2-2
LIBRARY OF CONGRESS CONTROL NUMBER: 2021949930

The Meadow and the Misread is set in Minion Pro

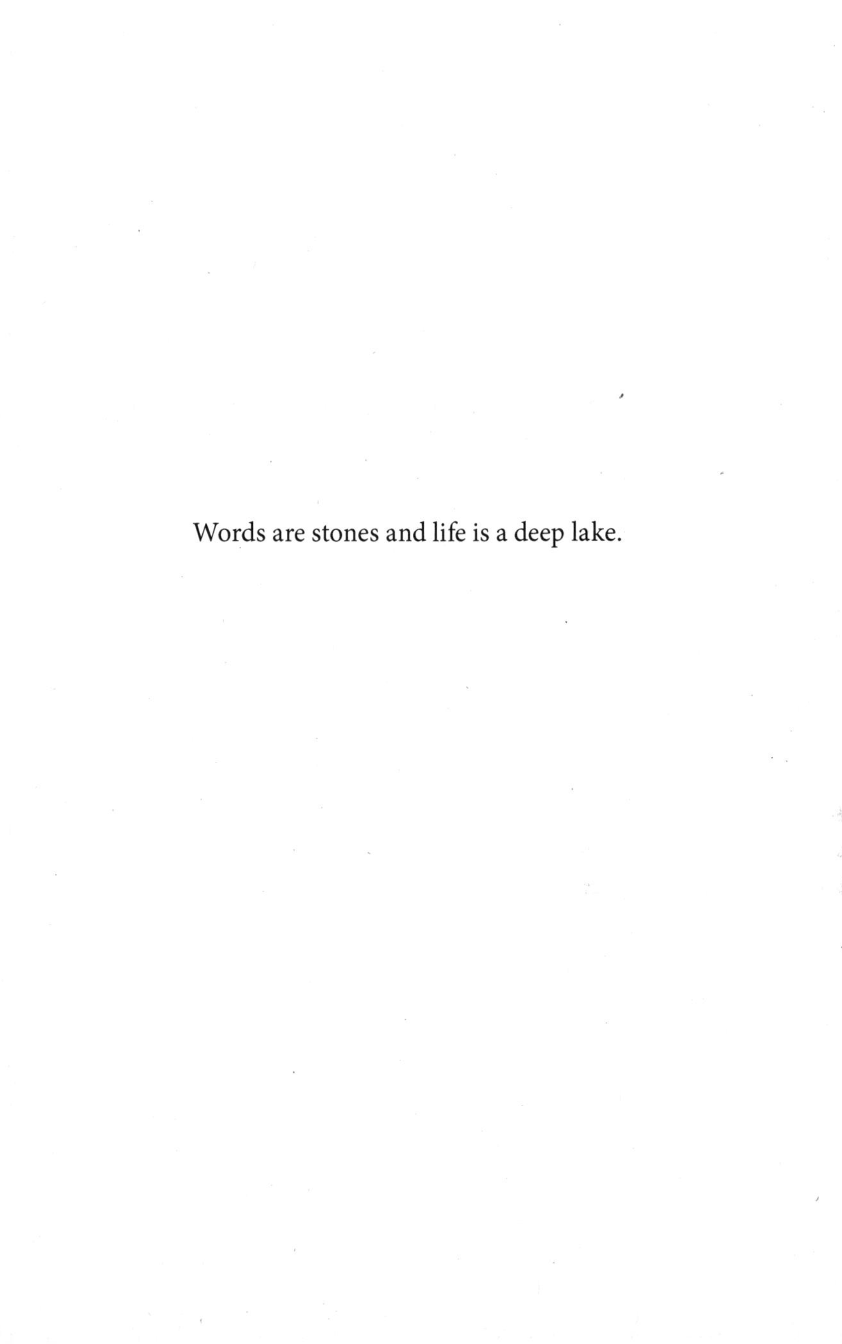

Words are stones and life is a deep lake.

PART 1

The Stalker

1

And so it is that one night during her first week of college, while playing a round of Never Have I Ever with her roommate and another girl from down the hall in which the Never Have I Evers amount only to very mild probing such as for example "Never have I ever eaten food out of the trash," or "Never have I ever farted in front of a boy," X Parke Penate arrives at the troubling realization that she does not remember anything from before the age of twelve or thirteen. There is a noticeable hardening of her expression and upturning of her hands and audible exhalation not unlike the gesture a person might make when having lost the glasses that were just a second ago on their face, and the roommate and the girl from down the hall, who are both named Jessa, exchange looks or a look that effectively communicates a mutual acknowledgment that this chick X Parke, who they hardly know, is very apparently experiencing some kind of physical or emotional or psychic anguish and they—the Jessas—need to be on guard because this X Parke chick looks suddenly like some central component of her self is unraveling and should she snap and start like trying to bite or gouge the Jessas then the Jessas need to have each others' backs because that's what Jessas do. But X Parke's hands alight to her knees and she works the bottom half of her face into something approximating a grin and goes, "You know? I don't know, actually," which at first to the Jessas amounts to gibberish until they realize she's responding to the prompt "Never have I ever seen my dad's penis," and the Jessas shrug and say "That's okay," because it's just a stupid game anyway, and they all sip their Hammond's Hard Ciders and X Parke nods at a vacant area of the dorm room as if at someone explaining to her a particular and urgent set of instructions.

2

Post a semester's worth of Humanities requisites and microwaveable mac-n-cheese, late-night partying and all-night studying and a dorm-wide outbreak of mono and one especially cringe-worthy sexual encounter with a boy who prematurely ejaculated in his hands the moment she gave consent, X Parke takes her finals and submits her final papers and asks a Jessa to drive her to the airport where she boards a flight north to spend the holidays with her family from who she feels—as she entwines her fingers in her lap and squints out the plane's scuffed plastic aperture at a crenulated terrace of white clouds churning and whipping below—distinctly very distant and disconnected and for some reason that likely pertains to the distinct distance and disconnection she's nervous to see them. From behind the curtain that cordons coach from first class there's a crash and laughter. X Parke acculturates to the plane's engine's thundering and the aggressive kerosene's odor and reflects for the first time in weeks on the problem of her memory or lack of memory, attempting again to recall anything that predates twelve or thirteen and still unable and so returning to the very first memory she *can* access, again circa twelve or thirteen, which is from her bed in her bedroom at home, on her side or else on her back with her neck twisted to her left so she's looking toward the room's door which is all the way open but there's nothing beyond meaning probably the hallway's dark rather than there being or not being some void beyond her bedroom—or perhaps simply her memory does not extend that far—and on her side or back looking at the door and then turning her body or head so that her chin is flush against her clavicle and her gaze is swooping down the length of her body where her feet beneath the fuzzy blanket always folded at the foot of her bed are vertical and extend up like fence posts so the blanket suspends in a gentle arc from foot to foot and in the dinge of either the bedroom or the memory the suspended blanket resembles a hedge somewhat, like what one may find cordoning one section of a garden from another or serving as the perimeter of a maze, and in X Parke's memory this hedge of blanket at the foot of the bed conceals the area of the bedroom beyond the bed's base, which is only about three feet of floor space from bed to wall, another three feet of width, and then three feet from the tip of her feet or the top of the hedge to the floor, so just twenty-seven cubic feet of unaccounted for space, which as her breath tremors against the plane's window's plastic seems like a lot of volume there unaccounted for and which she remembers as a twelve or thirteen year old imagining from her bed being occupied or infested by something she could not see by design. She remembers angling her feet outward so the blanket cambered downward revealing a newfound inch or two into the unseen space, revealing nothing but air and the shadowy wall, and X Parke being unable to look away from the area just where the blanket curved along the air, her gaze serving to hold at bay some idea of something, as if were she to look away then whatever was obviously *not* actually squatting there at the foot of her bed just beneath the hedge would suddenly materialize and spring up and menace her or else harm her in some way that twelve or thirteen year old X Parke felt, at twelve or thirteen, too young to imagine though she *could* imagine that there was some unimaginable threat here or elsewhere and that someday she would be old enough to imagine it and maybe even confront it face-to-face, or face-to-whatever constituted its face. The plane wobbles and X Parke's ginger ale dances. Part of deciding to travel home now when most of her new college friends are opting to stay on campus over break and continue the bonding ritual underway among the college's freshman is in order for X Parke to disclose to her family this problem of her memory or lack of memory and inquire as to whether they may be aware of it and/or its causes. Though it's difficult to say if she's overreacting, but memory loss or the altogether nonformation of memory is indicative as far as X Parke understands of an array of possible serious illnesses—and here X Parke swallows some ginger ale just as the plane again wobbles or shutters, the ginger ale sloshing onto her chin and neck, which she ignores—and concludes that if anything she has *under*reacted and should have made a phone call home or to a doctor about it back in September when she first became aware of the memory problem because what if there is something wrong with her brain going untreated—right?—like a degenerative brain thing, though the issue with this being that wouldn't her memory be getting worse though of course the brain is a strange and weird place and who knows how brain disease might decide to manifest in each and any given individual? And here again the plane shutters or really seems to drop hundreds of feet out of the sky before leveling off, the fingernails of the woman next to X Parke finding X Parke's forearm and a shriek or a sneeze from elsewhere in the plane's cabin and something like—and here X Parke cranes her ear forward—like chanting from first class, beyond the curtain. The woman next to X Parke's apologizing about the length of her tennis ball-green nails while little white crescent-shaped glyphs materialize across the outside of X Parke's forearm and a flight attendant scurries toward the front of the plane and passes through the curtain into first class and as the curtain flutters X Parke glimpses a pale face with pink eyes inset high up it, poised over a seatback grimacing back into coach which triggers X Parke to struggle to transmit the right signals from brain to throat for a few seconds during which her saliva pools in the little sublingual ditches—which feel quite huge in her mouth here—and overflows around her molars' trunks before the curtain straightens and the pale face is hidden and in X Parke's brain transforms into just a normal human face delivering a normal human expression and there's nothing wrong, and the saliva goes mostly down.

"I knew I should have driven," says the woman next to her, smoothing her blondish hair. "Lately every time I fly there is turbulence. It used to be that planes *wanted* to fly, I feel, but now it is a chore for them."

There is some kind of commotion from the front of coach, nearer the curtain, involving a child's voice and an adult male's voice in which the child's voice demands what sounds like "More hands," and the adult male's voice asserts "You've got enough hands,"—this being X Parke's approximation of the commotion's content, X Parke being too faraway and too inundated by the plane's engine's roaring—which seems to have regressed to just-pre-take-off volume—to clearly make out. That plus the chanting in first class, which is definitely chanting. The plane rattles a sort of winding sentence, and there are bubble-wrappy movements underfoot, punctuated by the FASTEN SEATBELT indicator's chirp. X Parke tightens her already fastened belt, thinks to finish her ginger ale and crush the plastic cup into the seatback slot and secure her tray table, then entwines her fingers in her lap and squints down again at the terrace of white clouds, which seem to have neared, or to which *she* seems to have neared, and which appear now less cloud-like and more not unlike the snowy canopy of a forest. And maybe it's exhaustion secreting whatever chemicals it's made of or else some larger existential machinations churning hard in the boiler room of her brain but suddenly—as in from one second to the next—looking down at the hilly clouds or snowy forest, X Parke feels like she wouldn't mind going down there and sitting peacefully there for awhile or forever, just dropping out of the plane and drifting down and landing softly on the soft white whatever, maybe sitting cross-legged with her hands upturned on her knees and her eyelids drawn halfway, just smiling or grinning or not smiling or grinning at all because the joy of such a descent is too divine or too profound to reduce to a facial expression, and the only appropriate way to express her bliss there atop the fuzzy blanket of clouds of forest would be to peel off her skin and bask her very skull in the burning sunlight. And she wouldn't mind just going down there at all, which is very excellent timing given now how the plane drops and lurches hard right or left, it's hard to say, but nonetheless lurches in some direction other than forward, which to X Parke's casual knowledge of flight physics is the only direction in which a plane should travel while airborne. And so here the plane is lurching hard let's say left, and at the same time listing right, so through the scuffed window now there's just cloud forest, no sky, and there are nails again perforating X Parke's forearm, shrieks ricocheting around the cabin and an overhead bin delatching and vomiting suitcases into the aisle, X Parke's head back against the headrest and her eyeballs feeling sucked upward as the plane drops now, plummets, the FASTEN SEATBELT's indicator chirping hysterically on and off, a flight attendant now bursting through the curtain and cart-wheeling down the aisle, a bundle of navy and skin, disappearing into the back of the plane, and there's smoke gushing like light through the whipping curtain, white and black and gathering first along the ceiling then toward the plane's left as the plane continues to list rightward until it feels upside down, a bat suddenly dangling here in front of X Parke's face which immediately she registers as an oxygen mask but can't help thinking of as a bat as now pale flames lap around the curtain's edges and the plane's engine roars brutally—and the still audible chanting the *chanting* what on earth?—the woman next to X Parke's nails now so deeply imbedded in X Parke's flesh that it actually starts to feel good, tasting the ginger ale returning from the dead of her stomach and the engine's roar crescendoing through the boundary of sound into a pall of blinding light and angry, acrid wind filling the cabin and roughhousing X Parke's hair all over. A small bird darts past her face. Her eyeballs feel too big for their sockets, and tumble in circles, clock the window where now all is blue, clock the woman next to her ragdolling in her seat and similarly blue, clock the curtain spasming there at the front of coach, no longer cordoning coach from first but cordoning coach from the expansive white terrace of clouds or forest toward which the plane curls, swallowing panes of abrasive menthol air that trellis and taper X Parke's consciousness into a dingy pocket of brown silence—then torn out into sunlight, wrenched from her seat and suspended here, for a moment held, as the world sways and turns below, falling just a ways and landing soft, her knees folding and her self folding down onto her back with her neck twisted to the side where a curve of white against a blue sky presents a sputtering sun, and for a long time she blinks into the sun until it slinks below the white's arc and even then she thinks about it, the sun, burning and thrashing below the horizon, squatting just below, ready to spring back up the instant she looks away and overwhelm the sky with light. Then X Parke's body—or just X Parke, depending on your definition—sinks back-first into whatever it is on which she's been placed, or on which she's landed, again, depending on your definition, until she is sucked down totally without any effort to slow or interrupt this descent into a harder underplace like pipes, tumbles, not at all gently now, snapping and bouncing from one to another and here landing on hard damp earth, a minute unfurling before shakily rising onto knees and eyes rolling up at the burning sun which has been waiting for her down here in the forest all along.

But it's not. It's formerly the fuselage, presently a tower of smoke and fire, fifty yards over there through the crowds of trees, the fire deforming the trees into quavering mockeries. X Parke watches. She's not convinced of something, or of anything at all. There are tennis ball-green fingernails sticking out of her forearm, she discovers, out of the skin like inflamed hairs or the eggs that protrude from the backs of certain frogs and insects. She works them out one by one, squeezing each by its root and wiggling or wriggling each free and leaving these crescent-shaped bloodless ditches arranged in a larger composite crescent along her skin. She wonders, the fuselage spattering and extravasating panes of terrible heat, how on earth she made it all the way to college before discovering this chasm in her pre-twelve or -thirteen memory. How does this happen to a person? What does it say about what may or may not have happened to X Parke, specifically insofar as the nature of a possible instigating factor that either erased or otherwise stunted her brain's memory-forming faculties to begin with, which with a surprising convulsion as one may exhibit when starting from sleep before a fall, X Parke is forced to consciously accede, as a blister of molten metal snaps off the fuselage and sets small fires on the near trees' outspread branches, that the dreaded T-word may be here in play. X Parke Penate never imagined this for herself, though probably neither do any who find themselves face-to-face or face-to-whatever with the prospect of having suppressed T and for that matter a T so T-tizing that its suppression eradicates a whole precious two-thirds of a life's memories. So X Parke turns this over, her body's front hot by the fiery wreck and her body's back cold by the frozen dark forest which she has yet to sort of acknowledge other than by name. There's no reasonable way to deny or dismiss the possibility of T, so much so that X Parke is embarrassed that it took her all the way to *here* before admitting its likelihood, because X Parke is smart, she knows, about a lot of things, but exceedingly stupid about others, stupider than people like Jessa—both Jessas—about whose characters X Parke considers carefully curated stupidity a central component. But likely the moment she mentioned to the Jessas this memory problem back in September—assuming she did, she does not remember mentioning it outright—even the Jessas probably right away concluded the likely presence of T as a culprit, probably talked about it or are talking about it right now in their special language of eyebrows and nostril flares, talking about X Parke's T generally since they cannot possibly know the T's specific nature but just that it exists. On the other hand X Parke's family may well and likely do know the T's specific nature, which raises a whole cascading slew of additional concerns, namely why they've withheld from X Parke the existence of T and what this might mean about the T's origins—all contingent of course on the existence of T to begin with, which, as the fuselage's complete right section bulges and oozes onto the forest floor and vines of fire grope up along the near trees' trunks, X Parke commands herself to stop assuming, since assumption has never gotten anyone—especially her—anywhere.

Which is why it's important now for her to get home and speak to her family about all this, because there's no sense in speculating further around the memory problem or possible T until she's gotten a bit more information. For all she knows her family will patiently assure her that she does, in fact, have memories from before the age of twelve or thirteen, a whole rich province of memories she's merely forgetting or ignoring and needs only a reminder, a word or an object—a toy, she thinks, turning 45° away from the wreckage—or an aroma or some other Proustian stimulus to sort of throw back or tear down the curtain cordoning her from her memories, yes *her* memories—and here her fist balls and perspiration gasps from the side of her body facing the fuselage, the left side—because if they are not *her apostrophe s*'s then they are no one's and nothing . . . though and here she continues another 45° so her back is toward the heat and her front cools rapidly in the total forest's dark, what if though the numeration of her life did not even *commence* until twelve or thirteen, meaning the span from zero to twelve or thirteen is merely a radix in the base of X Parke and so it isn't that there are no memories but rather no life to remember at all? X Parke smiles here into the dark forest at the sheer utter asininity of the prospect and continues the remaining 90° so she is once again face-to-face with the sputtering molten globule writhing among the onlooking crowds of backlit trees, having some sense of the magnitude here as wintry air sings through her clothes and onrushes the fuselage's abominable heat where invisibly the two states clash at the forest's dark midpoint, halfway between X Parke and the fuselage, icy wind vs fiery calefaction, the battlefront too dynamic and infinitesimal for her oafish eyes though she swears she tastes or smells the kaleidoscopic array of this soulless thermic confrontation, like roused prisms dripping with wax, and she fears she's probably concussed.

3

In the first soupy wisps of morning the forest blues. The night was short somehow, and not hard. X Parke's moved nearer to the fuselage's now smoldering carcass for warmth, and secured her sleeveless hoodie's hood snugly around her face so she suspects she would look like a monk or some other cenobitic type were there anyone around to witness, which there decidedly is not, X Parke really increasingly feeling her total aloneness. There's been a terrible accident. There are always terrible accidents, but usually faraway, on their own, without bothering X Parke or involving her. But now the accident has transpired inside X Parke's jurisdiction, and this close-proximity accident has entirely different texture and color—it's red and black, in case you're curious—whereas the faraway accidents are typically clear and even when there's color it's muted, technicolor accidents, dare she say *quaint*, the way that steel-eyed coal miners in old sepia photographs seem only the facsimiles of real laborers with no inkling of agency or the pains of the actual day-to-day. X Parke studies the corridors of trees for the sunlight's source, which is to her right if she's facing the fuselage, meaning she needs to go straight to go north, which she predicts is the direction in which her home and her family await. By way of safety X Parke gathers wide berth between herself and the fuselage, cutting first hopefully due west for she counts a hundred fifty steps and then turning back north now with the only fuselage-related obstacles the runnels of melted and rehardened metal of the fuselage's casing that tendril between the roots and rocks and which X Parke wonders, stepping over and around them lest they are not totally cooled, whether if she were to pry one up and flip it over if it would display an indentation of the forest's floor, the roots and rocks and even more malleable detritus like leaves and here are some mushrooms, an aluminous impression, and she starts to stop to do so but decides that probably there's risk involved, for example the metal still being hot since though it really does seem hardened it may still be very hot, hundreds of degrees, and were X Parke to scald herself out here at this point, having gotten as lucky as she appears to have gotten all things considered, well that would suck, basically, suck bad, and even if the metal's cool enough to touch there may be other dangers, unimaginable dangers, which try as she might X Parke cannot, by definition, plan for. So she steps over and around the runnels of hardened molten fuselage and pushes on into the lightening forest with her hood up and the further she gets from the wreckage the snowier the ground and the icier the trees' trunks and branches and sunlight coruscates until before long she's compelled to literally stop and gape at the crystalline lucence and marvelous architectonics of the forest's shape. Patternless, she thinks, shrugging as if in another context, profoundly ordered in its utter patternlessness. Hence is nature? But X Parke knows of patterns in nature, of symmetry; i.e. honeycombs, and fractal broccoli to name a couple, and the Rorschach of butterflies' wings. Snowflakes. X Parke's hands, for example, more or less, are inclined to symmetry when held together. But the forest resists this inclination. Beautiful anarchy, X Parke thinks, continuing now in this train of thought and northward through the canted trees and the topography's arrhythmia, categorizing everything she can think of into either PATTERNED or UNPATTERNED, krrching snow underfoot and so distracted by this classificational endeavor that she doesn't even realize she's being followed.

This instinct or impulse to classify is inspired in part by Professor Mel Lane, X Parke's first semester's comp lit instructor, whose predilection for dichotomizing the world into dual chalk columns was surprisingly infectious to the extent that X Parke now often projects this dual-column interface over her line of sight or line of thought and to which she devotes a serious amount of time. This despite her initial suspicion that the productivity or usefulness of this categorization was weak to say the least, whereas the third week of class, as Professor Lane drew *another* pair of columns on the board at the top of which he wrote in his meticulous caps MORTALITY AVERSION and REPRODUCTIVE URGE and then proceeded to list examples or conditions of each below each's respective category as each appeared in Gardiner Blyth's *The Long*

Pig, of which they'd read a third at that point, X Parke was inclined then to gather her things and scuttle away, thinking there was no possibility that such a basic approach to such a convoluted and multivalent text would or ever could be remotely helpful. But for reasons mainly of not wanting to distract her classmates or insult her professor, who was a nice and sightly man with an apparent inexhaustible collection of paisley button-downs and fitted jeans, X Parke stayed put and even did her due diligence of note-taking, and it wasn't until that night or the next night, cross-legged on her dorm room's twin bed with a cup of lukewarm tea and Blythe's tome spread across her lap that the impact of this dichotomous mindset as applied to the text became apparent, whereas all of a sudden the book made more sense, or made sense in a more exciting way when broken in half thus, and X Parke *knew* Blythe then and knew him well and was persuaded and won over and began to actually giddily refer to herself in front of the Jessas as a Lane acolyte to the extent that the Jessas started teasing her about a crush that X Parke protested too adamantly and often. And it was true: Prof Lane was a stud, and a sneaky genius to boot, and X Parke found herself anticipating his T/R 9:00am-10:50am seminar with perhaps more than just the typical scholastic enthusiasm, and but found her mind and gaze less on the Blythe and increasingly on the paisley, which is why in October during a conference in Prof Lane's basement office with the attenuated windows near the office's ceiling bleeding pinched yellow light and Prof Lane's desk littered kind of prettily with fans of papers and tented books and folders,

Lane himself at the desk's opposite end with his legs neatly crossed and his paisley shirt's sleeves neatly rolled up his hirsute forearms, X Parke had made it a point to wear her own paisley skirt and paisley stockings and even a paisley t-shirt albeit under a plaid flannel but which she made sure to expose at the neck by way of unbuttoning the flannel's top buttons and had even shaved her legs just just just in case. All of this in retrospect, as bells chitter fitfully in the forficating sunlight and the forest lurks on, seeming to her quite puerile and obvious and pathetic, a pathetic attempt to attract the attentions of a man so outside of her proverbial league that she probably did not even register to him as a female and certainly not as a sexually available one. Prof Lane there in the office looking mostly down at the sheath of pages of X Parke's latest essay which X Parke could see from her side of the desk, as she undid another button on the plaid flannel, was veritably drenched in red marker, then drumming his wedding band on the desk's edge and saying, "You know miss Penate I don't know about this," gesturing vaguely at the essay, "I have reservations about this." X Parke fingering her paisley skirt, a bank of black hair curtaining an eye in a manner she hoped appeared even a quarter as alluring as it felt ungainly, then merely shrugging as Prof Lane slid the essay over the desk in her direction, gouged at it with index and middle wedged stiffly together and explained her assumptions, her misqualifications, the difference between authorial and narrative intent, how to use a semicolon, etc., X Parke kind of breathing calmly, kind of ironing her skirt over her thigh in case Lane hadn't noticed the paisley, the hair across her eye increasingly bewildering until she had no choice but to tuck it aside and show her face. Prof Lane meanwhile barely looking at her, just speaking toward her shit essay and basically growing a beard in front of her, the office's wall-mounted clock's legato second hand announcing the universe's silent and unrelenting expansion until finally X Parke took her essay and started the long exit from the small office, embarrassed and rebuffed and wearing way too much paisley, getting all the way to the door and turning the doorknob all the way before behind her Prof Lane went "I love that you love Blythe, but maybe consider that he doesn't love you so much yet."

Meanwhile the snow deepening here at the extreme depth of a wooded flume, X Parke in her old Converse having of course not planned to do much walking in the snow between airports, stepping gingerly and occasionally looking back over her shoulder at the lonely frozen woods, recalling the time she'd seen Prof Lane at a gallery in town one weekend evening with his wife, who of course was nothing short of ravishing with deepset virescent eyes and pixie-cut coral hair and a grownup woman's body that curled X Parke's toes in her high-top Converse, the two of them cradling clear plastic cups of yellowish wine and mouthing polysyllabic nothings beside a convex sculpture, X Parke having arrived with the Jessas and stealing furtive ogles through the forest of people across the gallery's length, inadvertently making eye contact with Prof Lane who blinked and looked away and placed his crinite hand on the profound crescent of his wife's waist, X Parke turning away and nervously chewing handfuls of mini-pretzels by the gallery's entrance while the Jessas explored and applied descriptive variations of *phallic* to the smattering of oil paintings on the gallery's first wall, X Parke paying attention to Prof Lane and Mrs. Prof Lane's orbit through the gallery and correlating her own position so to remain always antipode until the Lanes were then by the gallery's entrance/exit and X Parke found herself sort of timorous beside the convex sculpture whose dimensions made her feel like a child, watching the Lanes depart through a gale of handshakes and air-kisses until when just after Prof Lane ushered his wife through the door he turned back and looked at her, X Parke, and he nodded and then jerked or gestured with his head toward the door before exiting into the night. X Parke left then categorizing the head's gesture's potential intent into two columns: either THIS IS SOMETHING MY HEAD DID BY ACCIDENT or COME HITHER, MISS PENATE and finding the likelihood of such a discrete and specific gesture being anything other than the latter unlikely—especially from a man as discerning as Prof Mel Lane—her heart then doing an abrupt pirouette as she essed through the gallery's denizens and out onto the November's night's sidewalk and saw them there a block down arm-in-arm, strolling through the streetlamps' columns of auburn light, X Parke drawing up her hood and following them through town and into the park, their voices like wind chimes from the path ahead as X Parke worked out how this was going to go, anticipating what might be expected of her here and demanding of herself she not simply give consent but rather proclaim enthusiasm when the inevitable question arose, the question's content still mysterious to X Parke but not for long as Prof and Mrs. Lane exited the park's east entrance and turned south toward the row of stout brownstones on Castle Street, X Parke turning after them and wondering if there even would be a question or if it would just happen—or if it was happening already—and that for all that was holy if she could just manage to get through it with some grace and tact . . . unless of course grace and tact were not what the Lanes expected or desired from her, this for which there was some persuasive evidence insofar as X Parke having been chosen out of anyone to join them, and maybe what they sought from her was the awkwardness and inexperience—the girl not the woman—that Prof Lane undoubtedly associated with her, and did it matter if she knew either way because what discipline did X Parke possess over her own constitution? Then Prof and Mrs. Lane were climbing the steps of a brownstone at the block's end, pausing on the landing to fish for keys, and X Parke slowed still several houses back and drew the hood from her face to look up at the landing better where Mrs. Lane's laughter was like glass bells and Prof Lane was smiling—X Parke had never seen his face do this, and was unsure about how it made her feel—his eyes creased and then his eyes finding X Parke's and hardening and the smile sinking into the crevice of his teeth and a deep hole fell open in the sidewalk beneath X Parke's Converse and she fled back through the park and through the town and to the dorm and curled onto her twin bed and read Blythe, since it was, as Prof Lane had pointed out, *Blythe* that she loved, and *Blythe* who was available to her, and she was just grateful to Lane for having properly introduced them and had merely misconstrued that gratitude with affection in her stupid little brain.

Bells meanwhile flitter through the forest, X Parke only just noticing them now or just noticing that she's noticed them and stopping halfway up a steepish incline to listen to and scan the oblique forest through her breath, clocking nothing obvious as the bells' source given the thoroughly inorganic character of the bells or of bells in general and the forest conversely a dense byword of nature. The sun now somewhere high eastish parading as vague, smoky light through the canopy, the bells sort of receding or stilling and X Parke continuing on up the slope and over a mound of snow that may be a fallen tree or a long boulder, soon hearing the bells resume and abruptly pivoting and seeing there some twenty yards away among the arcade of icy trees a person standing sort of agley and akimbo with one hand's tennis ball-green fingernails fanned across its face. X Parke shakes her head as if at an offensive solicitation, gasps and then covers her mouth with both hands like a child who's just swore in front of a teacher while a clump of snow shakes loose on its own from a tall branch and plummets silently. The person sways then as if in a wind and dances jerkily toward X Parke with a clattering of bells, X Parke recoiling instinctually and her Converse sliding on a swatch of ice and her legs splaying, taking a knee and starting to rise but finding the person approaching much too quickly—for the terrain namely, but also for a person generally, seeming merely to skim across the ground—and so X Parke stays down and upturns both hands like as if for alms and in a gesture that she prays connotes passivity. The person then kind of rocking to a stop five or ten yards away, the tennis ball-green fingernailed hand obscuring the face, but X Parke recognizes the outfit and the blondish hair and especially the fingernails and gasps again, this time with relief, overwhelmed at the appearance of anything familiar out here in the trackless forest to the point that she could literally cry. The person or the woman from the next seat then waving her other hand flaccidly, the one missing its fingernails, and saying, "Aren't we cold?" in a different voice than the voice X Parke remembers as the one belonging to or coming out of the woman on the plane, it being instead papery and breathless and lurching from tree to tree, and X Parke notices also now the woman's shoes are not, actually, touching completely the forest's floor at all but rather dangling there scarcely brushing it. Moreover she looks bad, sick or something, whereas what little of her face X Parke can glean peeking through the hand is as pale as the forest and the hand's skin itself paler still, and the clothes are torn and scuffed and the right leg is bent incongruously out over the knee, and X Parke kind of scoffs and blinks at the woman's torpefied body where also it looks like strings or wires are fastened to and extending up from its wrists and ankles and the top of its head toward the forest's shadowy ceiling where after drawing back her hood to better trace the wires' path X Parke discerns at their terminus and barely perceptible a raggy figure perched in the forest's rafters. And it is here that whatever is suspending the body barks, "*Aren't we?*" from the branches and titters the body so it emulates grotesquely the last time X Parke saw it, ragdolling in the seat beside her as the plane dove out of the sky, the tennis ball-green fingernailed hand jostling briefly aside so that the face is revealed, and the hole in the face where the left eye and cheek should be so deep and dry that X Parke is reminded of the passage in *The Long Pig* in which Blythe describes the well on the property that Joseph Shapiro discovers many impractical acres from the house and looks down into and espies or thinks he espies another well at its bottom, and at that well's bottom another and onward down into 'relentless consequence,' X Parke having circled and underlined and asterisked this passage nearly pathologically, it seeming at the time of her reading to contain profound truths correlated to Prof Lane's most recent dichotomy—DEATH and DYING—only to arrive at class the morning following and tear into this expansive explication of her findings which when she finally looked up at her classmates inferred uncomfortably had amounted to inanity or even gibberish and then had blushed and shrugged and Lane had called on someone else. Now as the hand's tennis ball-green fingernails relinquish their position before the face's hole and the whole body hovers up a yard over the forest's floor and rattles and bells crash everywhere, X Parke dashes left and zags through trees and vaults over a snowy chine and down the palm of a slick embankment, thudding out of a fall so her breath's smacked cleanly away from her, scrambling up and running now, running through snow the snow clawing at her Converse and her lungs panicking, bells pealing behind and beside her, not stupid enough to turn around but too stupid to plan her trajectory so slipping and sliding now and prostrate, the bells also laughing, X Parke's thoughts spinning out toward again Blythe's evocation of the well as 'desperately venerable, hand-scored and head-carven,' on which Prof Lane had quite a bit to say, an interesting take, on the archaic past participle—Blythe being still alive now and well, or alive as far as anyone knows—and also how it correlated to some stuff toward the chapter's latter. Also that day he'd done a lot of standing at the chalkboard, Lane, and his paisley was particularly svelte, X Parke in the auditorium's second row with her Blythe in her lap, now sliding belly-first over ice and colliding with a flat and hard thing, Prof Lane drawing his columns though X Parke cannot remember what each's label was that day as she turns now and looks up at a pitted surface which, blinking and rising, she discovers is the outer wall of an old limekiln here at the forest's gut, towering up through the ramous branches, with an X Parke-sized hole in its side as if blasted there—maybe LIMINAL and ABSOLUTE—and so drawing herself up and scrambling through the limekiln's hole as the bells encroach, feeling a rent at her calf and crab-walking across the limekiln's interior's triturated floor until her back is on the far cold wall and staring ahead through bars of black hair at the hole through which the white forest creaks.

Or not LIMINAL and ABSOLUTE but FLUIDIC and STAGNANT X Parke recalls as a shadow blesses the kiln's threshold and the bells reverberate in and up the kiln's shaft and bat around its somber top, and here now the body swoops and dangles outside the threshold, baying "*Cold girl! Cold Girl!*" kicking and beating its soft limbs in. X Parke mitigates her panic by entwining fingers in lap. The body comes no further or cannot come further than the threshold and anon the beating flags and the limbs pendulate and the body crumples onto the snow irregularly, head wilting and wrists readjusted so the hand's tennis ball-green fingernails entwine with the others hand's and it is still and the wires slacken and the bells peter out into just glassy birdsong far off. One thing X Parke's still confused about as it pertains to her entanglement with Prof Mel Lane is what he'd meant in that case then with his head jerk or gesture at the gallery if not as a signal for X Parke to follow, since such a gesture's implication is tricky to otherwise interpret. Which leaves two possibilities in X Parke's mind: 1) that the jerk or gesture never happened and X Parke imagined it or saw something other than what had occurred in actuality, though this hardly makes sense given her eidetic recollection of the moment and Lane's aloof eye-contact and the precision of the gesture etc., or 2) that the jerk or gesture *had* occurred and *had* intended to signal X Parke to follow or come with and *had* denoted all the things X Parke inferred only to then have Lane change his mind at some point between the gallery's exit and the front steps of his and his wife's brownstone, meaning X Parke had merely accurately interpreted signals and obediently followed instruction and had not assumed or misread but rather it was Prof Lane who was confused and who thought he wanted something he didn't want or wanted something he decided he couldn't have and in this more credible plausibility it was him and not X Parke who was the—

"What are we thinking, cold girl?"

X Parke here blinking back at the body folded on the feculent snow, the voice having come from just outside and above the limekiln's threshold, that same papery, dead-leaf voice, and X Parke unentwines her fingers and sets her palms on her thighs and the body unentwines its fingers and flaps its palms onto its lap. There is an odor in the limekiln, X Parke decides, of chalk.

"What are we thinking?" the body's head jerking minutely.

X Parke upturns her hands and shrugs, "Nothing," and notices then just barely breaching the threshold's upper edge a nest of dark brindle from which glisten an exacting pair of pupil-less animal eyes.

"We think nothing all the time," the voice fingers into the kiln, "intractable meadows of nothing. Often we think so much nothing it starts to feel like *some*thing. Do we know what this's like, cold girl? Does this remind us of anything?"

X Parke genuinely considers this question despite her suspicion that it's duplicitous or otherwise spurious at its root, thumbing through her rolodex for a comparable experience and finding herself once again face-to-face with the unmitigated pre-twelve or -thirteen void, again forced to reckon with its implications and literally shuddering as again the possibility of some very severe T rears up and obscures the sun and casts a long headless shadow at

X Parke's feet, and she draws her feet up and folds her legs beneath her and shakes her head and says, "I don't know."

Wires adjust the body's legs and judder the head as the forest's light leans now aslant through the limekiln's threshold, milkening its dusty interior. Just a couple days ago X Parke'd gone to leave her final essay in the dropbox mounted on the wall outside Prof Lane's office, and it was getting late—not quite 10pm but coming on that, X Parke having had a fuck of a time getting the thing written—so the Academic Arts Building was quiet and differently lit than she was used to whereas entire corridors receded into shadow and her own shadow wrinkled along the wall as if underfed, arriving at AAB238 and finding the dropbox already choked with essays and the office door shut but from its seam white light leaking and beyond it stifled voices, X Parke looking back at the darkened hallway and then tucking her hair behind her ear and pressing her ear against the door's cold surface, the lobe suctioning to the door's aluminum and the office's voices deepening and droning, two voices or three punctuated by a female's voice, breathless, and something toppling and scattering, X Parke's palms flush on the door's frame, listening to the voices through the aluminum and the tide of her brain's blood, compelled for some unfathomable reason then to kiss the door softly and instantly embarrassed despite her solitude, withdrawing her head from the door and her hands from the frame only in doing so just idiotically clicking her fingernails on the door at which point the chanting abruptly ceased, and there was only the susurrus of the building's old radiators and X Parke sort of stricken there unknowing whether to flee or not or to just dematerialize somehow, though then for a moment it seemed like it didn't matter because nothing was happening and the shadows bent through the hallway and the radiators whispered and she was about to turn and go when AAB238's door swung back and light roared onto her and seized her wrist and dragged her forward all in one eruptive instant, and then X Parke with her black hair and her favorite hoodie off which she'd cut the sleeves—and which she's wearing now too—was in Lane's office again, and there was Lane at his desk with his chair drawn prudely under and his hands folded on top, looking down at his lap it seemed, or at something under his desk, and the door cracked shut behind X Parke and she looked from her arm to her wrist to the enormous and floridly tattooed hand clamped there and up the hand's suit sleeve and to the wide face attached, a grinning face with deep coulees like the skin of a tree and generous gaps between the amber teeth and eyes heavily top-sanpaku and white hair ponytailed away from the endless forehead, this face branding itself into X Parke's memory there in Lane's office just like that and X Parke not even really trying to dislodge her wrist from the hand whose grip was so absolute that it would have been, she imagined, like trying to tear her very body from the unforgiving velocity of time itself. X Parke then looking between Lane and this other man and stuttering cartoonishly an apology in which only the first and last syllables of her words managed to land, her throat suddenly very dry. "One of ours?" the man then saying, his voice shockingly bassy, still grinning at X

Parke so for a moment she thought he was asking her, then Lane nodding minutely at his desk, his head still bowed, and there was a tsk behind X Parke and she started to turn to see who else was in the room but the man's grip tightened and he drew her toward him and said, "Is it nosy?" and X Parke tried to swallow and said, "No," and the man winked and said, "Yes," and carved his dark tongue along his incisors' crests, his huge eyes some indiscernible shade, and said "Let's check inside at our investment" and X Parke could merely look at Lane, or at the top of Lane's head as he continued to face downward, so bent over his desk his nose skimmed the desk pad, and she clocked for the first time a faint clearing on his scalp where his hair was starting to thin and had a distinct and startling realization that this man about whom she'd spent so many nights beneath the sheets of her dorm room's twin bed frantically pawing at herself over was *not* the man she thought he was or at least the one she wanted him to be, cowering here in his own office, and X Parke almost sneered but did not want to be derisive, since it wasn't Lane's fault he was losing his hair, and the man with the tattooed hands meanwhile breathing palls of tobacco-breath into X Parke's face, X Parke knowing she should be saying something assertive and keen, threatening to kick the man's shin or file a Title IX complaint or whatever, and but yet could not manage to do or say anything, something about this man so arresting that even her brain's cylinders were kind of cowed, and the man snorted and winked again only this time over X Parke's head and his mouth opened and his lips flexed and a white shape ballooned from his mouth and floated in front of his face, then another shape and another and they hung there in the air in a line like glyphs in some impenetrable phrase and there was rustling behind X Parke and something covered her face, a red cloth that smelled like wet dirt, and X Parke thrashed and but futilely, the cloth constricting around her face until it turned black and something bony and oily flapping against her head, and there was thunderous laughter as if faraway and X Parke felt herself suddenly upside-down, or sideways, or backwards maybe, and but regardless suspended and turned around and there were voices, indiscernible, and X Parke was again on her feet and the cloth rippled and reddened and was gone, and the man's wide face creasing and his colorless eyes swaying between Lane and X Parke as if watching a tennis match, nodding then and saying, "Carry on," and leaving then in a singular motion, neglecting to close Lane's office's door and leaving X Parke and Lane alone then in AAB238 with X Parke's hair scrambled about her face, smoothing it and smoothing her hoodie and the ankle-length skirt beneath, Lane leaning back then in his chair and kneading his face and sighing thrice and looking at X Parke and pursing his lips and going merely, "Sssss . . ." and X Parke sighed too and said, "Who *was* that?" and Lane frowned and said, "The Dean," and X Parke nodded, waited, said, "Are you okay?" and Lane's eyes bleared and he rolled down the sleeves of his paisley shirt and buttoned them and said, "Yes," and X Parke placed the heel of one Converse against the toe of the other and looked at the clock on the wall over the desk and said, "My paper's in the dropbox. I . . . it was hard . . . anyway. Thanks for everything. I learned a lot," and then turned and started into the hallway, Lane's voice then stopping her in the doorway, "Miss Penate," and she turned.

"Yes?"

"Good work this semester."

And X Parke smiled and walked back across campus to the dorms where the party was just revving up and found the Jessas wasted and dancing in the quad and X Parke'd danced with them in the kind of dead-armed shuffle-step dance she never brought out in public but in this case was just genuinely thrilled to be done with her first semester of college and underway with her actual life and therefore uninhibited and also tired enough not to care.

"Give us back what we took though," the voice points up.

X Parke blinks around the limekiln's dingy interior. "I didn't take anything from you."

The body's hands upthrust to either side of its head, one with tennis ball-green fingernails and the other without, and X Parke glances at her forearm, where the crescent-shaped ditches have made no effort to close, and reaches into the front pocket of her hoodie and cups the fingernails there and holds them out in an upturned palm toward the limekiln's threshold. The body's fingernail-less hand upturns in the same manner as X Parke's and the voice says, "Put them here, if you don't mind," and X Parke hesitates, recalling the now distant first day she attended Prof Lane's class in September wearing shorts for the heat and sitting in the front row and seeing him arrive in his paisley and place his papers on the lectern and erase the chalkboard of its previous class's errata and then turn to the class and see X Parke there, his eyes flickering across her legs and then away and motioning vaguely at the auditorium's second row and saying, "Sit back there, if you don't mind," X Parke then as now doing as she's told, feeling then as now as if something's going wrong, taking her seat in the second row, the seat that would become her only seat all semester though she never wore shorts to his class again or at all really since then, now craning out her arm toward the body's white palm, starting to place the nails on it as a thin line darts through the limekiln's threshold and curls around her wrist and fastens acutely there, her fingers involuntarily flexing and the tennis ball-green fingernails spilling, smelling the sunscreen's odor and the chalk's odor amalgamating that first day of class and Prof Lane's expressionless silence behind the lectern as the time beat slowly toward class's commencement, X Parke watching him cross to the auditorium's thermostat and alter it and return to the lectern and consider something, X Parke feeling the other students look between them and placing her folder across her lap as cold air breathed through the floor vents, the wire slicing into her wrist and drawing her inexorably toward the kiln's threshold where the glassy eyes do not blink or betray their focus, Lane's unsignified beckoning and the synaptic rustling of his papers, "Come here, cold girl . . ." and the furious lashing of bells. And here I allow X Parke into a sallow gray that is only to sleep as dying is to being dead, and I show myself, and though I cannot speak I *can* listen, and thereupon—when, soon after, the pupil-less eyes harden and withdraw, and the wire loosens from X Parke's wrist and there is rustling in the branches around the kiln and the body's wires tauten and the body trawls off across the frozen ground and disappears into the passages of white trees so that when X Parke comes to she is alone and after stretching her back and legs she continues on through the forest in the direction she hopes approximates the one in which her home is.

4

Somehow she's not as cold as she imagines she should be. She's trying to decide what exactly is happening when she exhales and sees her breath, meaning what exactly does her breath look like, if anything, and is it actually her breath she's seeing? Not that she doubts it's her breath, but rather she suspects she's not actually *seeing* it. The best she can tell, the breath refracts light but does not have its own color and is not otherwise obscuring or transmuting the appearance of anything, i.e. warping or magnifying, but only merely refracting light in a way that X Parke—the more she thinks about it—associates with the properties of a very clean window which though may be indistinguishable from its outlook is yet perceptible by its refraction of the light; here her breath twinkles, and yet through the pall of it the forest is unchanged. Refraction, she thinks, picking her way diagonally down a steep bank with the bonish trunks of juvenile birches or beeches for support, is unique to translucent phenomena. Or is it transparent? Or is refraction ubiquitous in seeing? Does everything refract light? Is that what color is? Is that how the world manifests fact and form?

X Parke's one semester of Humanities requisites did not include a science class, and nor would she have enjoyed one if she'd taken it, having always struggled with rote and mathematics. Which X Parke though understands is not implicit in *all* science classes, just most. In high school—which she remembers well—there had been bio and chem and physics, dreadful boring doodle-sessions, but there had also been a philosophy of science elective with Ms. Inoue, an exclusive bi-weekly class in the library's seldom-used conference room in which Ms. Inoue sat with her students at the semioval table and waxed fervently about the stranger potentialities of the natural sciences. For example stuff like the demarcation problem, and whether time has a quantum value or is merely the distance between events, and this really nifty idea about how given that when solid objects come into contact with one another some x number of atoms from each object pass beningly through the others so it therefore being theoretically possible that at some point the x atoms of either or both objects will be sufficient enough that said objects will simply swish right through, or that maybe it's already happened somewhere whereas X Parke imagines just two asteroids of the quadrillions scudding through the bleak bowels of space coming contingently together and merely silently breathing through each other and tumbling off as if neither was ever there and X Parke wonders now how many times she'd have to walk into a birch or beech before glitching through it, and for a not-entirely-brief moment fears that the x atoms of her feet might likely slip through the x atoms of the forest floor and she will plummet into the crushing furnace of the earth's middle. But this philosophy of science stuff X Parke found sort of endlessly fascinating because probably it felt so exo-high school, so much less "Here learn this" and so much more "Here think this over" which distinction had the unfortunate effect of making every other high school science class feel even more like forced labor than it already did. She mentioned this to Ms. Inoue, who was young for a high school teacher and skinny like X Parke and dressed well, the two of them having at least that much in common, and Ms. Inoue seesawed a hand like so and explained that she had been the same way when she was X Parke's age, sixteen or seventeen, and had really dreaded science classes and been generally off-put by the black and white way in which it was taught, being a person much more inclined to gray, and that it wasn't until college that she, Ms. Inoue, was introduced to thinking about science in a new light—a gray light—and learned about uncertainty in science and started to get excited about the things that were not known or not known for sure, which it turned out was virtually everything, and that helped make the rote and the math more interesting because it wasn't about memorizing the procedures for understanding how the thing worked every time, but about understanding the procedures enough to start to espy when the thing didn't work or might not work, and to learn to challenge the things that scientists traditionally referred to as *laws* but which Ms. Inoue encouraged X

Parke to start thinking more of as *tendency*. This all being the reason Ms. Inoue had wanted to bring a philosophy of science class to X Parke's high school, since while she was qualified to teach college and everyone in her life i.e. her parents and fiancé and mentors all encouraged her to teach college she felt deep down it was more important to teach this stuff to younger students some of whom, like X Parke, might be grappling with the value of science and she, Ms. Inoue, wanting to help those students discover why it was cool and fun. And maybe important, if X Parke was into that kind of thing. X Parke was, and paid attention to Ms. Inoue and stayed engaged in the elective, which proved ultimately to be the academic highlight—though not the overall highlight—of the 11th grade. Either way however X Parke never developed a taste for the rote and math, and after graduating and going to college and pursuing a humanities education, whatever inklings of excitement for science Ms. Inoue had stirred in her are now atrophied. And she doesn't understand light refraction. Or breath.

Now pausing at the peak of a scarped embankment pocked with lesions of icy roots and squinting out at where snowflakes pitch lethargically onto the expansive face of a patchily frozen lake. Low clouds rush over. And X Parke thinks about the shallow arching blanket at the foot of her bed, and she thinks about the green door in the back of the attic of her family's house half-concealed behind an old dresser, the door's green paint flaking in layers away from the raw wood, and the pulsing camps of sleeping bats she knows sleep beyond like uvulas in the dark mouth of the unfinished attic's north half, dripping from the rafters in the fitful dark. Occasionally one would find its way into the house proper and panic along the ceilings with schizophrenic predictability, threatening to entangle itself in hair and burrow into clothes. X Parke scans the lake's far shore through the snow, convincing herself she has the math to determine how long she'll spend on the fenestrated ice from here to there versus how long it will take to walk the lake's circumference and resume northward at the opposite point. The lake's surface so precariously moderately frozen and in some parts not frozen at all that X Parke thinks about the x atoms in her feet and how readily they would swish through the feeble ice and drag her down into the freezing unbreathable dark, and so she starts her way along the lake's eastern shoreline—the western shoreline is mostly slick-looking vertical rock face—which esses out of sight about a quarter mile up so that she really cannot accurately predict how long it will take her to get to the lake's north shore this way but has no alternative. Ms. Inoue often wore this green sweater dress for which it looked like she'd skinned a pool table, at first X Parke not understanding it or more specifically what Ms. Inoue was thinking with it but then over time coming to appreciate its sort of misshapen allure, the way sort of that Ms. Inoue alluded to her body by obscuring it rather than actually displaying it and how this was actually better because it gave the viewer an opportunity to imagine the body beneath which would always trump the real thing 100% of the time. Two columns: IMPLICIT and EXPLICIT. The same reason X Parke prefers reading to watching movies. It was clever technique from Ms. Inoue, in her baggy green sweater dress, and so X Parke adopted the style and then did it even better. X Parke's fashion generally is something she's very proud of. Usually a few sizes too big on top, lots of blacks with vibrant splashes of bright color, especially greens and reds. Like now in her sleeveless hoodie, which is black with an unidentified logo on the front, green blue red yellow, a thrift find like most things, and her black skinny jeans which are skinny jeans for someone a couple sizes up and on X Parke are just baggy enough to implicate her legs' shapes rather than explicate, and of course she loves long flowy skirts too but would never fly in one, now needing to cut some paces away from the lake's edge to bypass an indentation in the shoreline and cataloging the clothes she'd packed for the trip home which are now gone forever. X Parke's not particularly sentimental, and is cataloging not so much by way of mourning what's lost rather than to note what needs to be replaced if and when she should get the chance. It must be noon by now or later. The forest rustles to the right, X Parke's, something shuffling through the frozen brush. X Parke now turning and crouching to look through the knotty thuck of briar, expecting a deer maybe, or a large raccoon, maybe a fox would be cool, but seeing there instead a pair of pants with legs inside, tapered black pants sewn with polygonal patches of colored fabric like what might be a picnic blanket and maybe part of a bandana—even a lacy white diamond over the knee which is more likely than anything a swatch of wedding dress—and traffic cone-orange sneakers, and X Parke stands and leans to see around the briar and there's a boy, a young man X Parke's age or just older with wild black hair, his black Carhartt a size or three too big and fading along its creases and a white t-shirt under where a collection of vibrant necklaces at various lengths hang, necklaces made from plastic beads and bottlecaps and at least one that looks like Legos, and on the boy's throat there's tattooed a thick black spiral with the spiral's midpoint at his adam's apple and radiating to his jaw on the top and his clavicle on the bottom which X Parke is getting a good look at given the stretched elastic of his t-shirt's neck-hole. This boy's looking just at an obtuse enough angle that he doesn't see X Parke, but X Parke can see his eyes which are these explosive cerulean gems, and in which X Parke can actually make out the forest's white limbs and the tender lake and the tenderly crashing snow. And so giddy about this random cool boy and his magnificent eyes here in the forest's random middle, X Parke steps out and says "Hi," and even does this little wave from her chin that the Jessas always told her was super kawaii and so which X Parke makes sure to keep oiled.

The boy blinks and his eyes flash at X Parke, and from across the lake an enormous bird unfurls and batters its way into the low sky. The boy says, "Are you real?"

X Parke taking about two seconds too long to come up with a clever response and only going, "I think so."

The boy nods contemplatively as if X Parke's just given him a sequence of words and numbers to memorize, his staggering eyes now exploring X Parke from head to Converse. "I like your sweater," he says.

"I cut the sleeves off myself."

"I figured."

"I like your pants."

"I sewed this stuff on them."

"I see."

"You don't have any booze," just like that with no question mark.

X Parke shrugs. "No sorry."

The boy's lips purse and he squints off at the lake's far shore as it decays behind a thickening shroud of glassy mist. Something about the way he seems to be seeing stirs in X Parke this conviction that he's seeing what she's seeing—i.e. the view of the far shoreline—in the same way she is, which is not remarkable except that at the same time she becomes convinced that she has never shared with anyone the same sight in this way, whereas though having shared views with people before but yet always seeing the space differently, or from a different angle, or if from the same angle than from separate perspectives, namely HER PERSPECTIVE and THEIR PERSPECTIVE where the view's focus or the view's center may differ, or the view's periphery may start and end elsewhere, or even just something as vague and nebulous as the view's *feel* being just inherently *other*, in this case, with this boy, X Parke's convinced they are experiencing the same view and the same focus and that the view's periphery is mapped identically and they are *feeling* the same thing.

"So where did you come from?" the boy's eyes coruscate.

"My plane crashed," X Parke shrugging. "I'm trying to get to my family's home and I don't think it's far."

"Your plane crashed?"

"Yep."

"Like . . . crashed crashed?"

"Oh yeah."

"Are you sure you're real?"

X Parke smiling and tucking a bank of hair back. "As real as you."

The boy here extending a hand toward the lake palm-up and holding, X Parke noticing now a distinct tremulousness in the hand and looking away, feeling oddly as if she's just seen something she shouldn't have. "The snow's getting worse," the boy saying, withdrawing the hand and exhaling a plume of breath. "We should go inside."

"Inside where?"

"I'm posted up in this old place, just back there," pointing vaguely back. "It's big and empty so we wouldn't even have to see each other but it's warm and we'll be safe from the weather. I have food too, a little, and you can have some. You look hungry."

"I look hungry?"

"I mean, I don't know. I'm projecting," finger-gunning himself in the temple.

"Yeah."

Now shrugging his eyebrows, X Parke nodding and gesturing for him to go on, that she'll follow, turning briefly as they march into a thicker section of forest to look back again at the lake's far shoreline which in fact is now gone behind a wall of white and where the nearer section of lake she can still see is no longer patchy but frozen solid across and gathering irregular mounds of snow, turning and hurrying to keep up with this boy who's also sewn a patch onto the back of his Carhartt she can now see of what's like an old Japanese woodcarving of a tsunami menacing a blotch of land with a few bonsai-looking trees, and X Parke follows him closely trying—she realizes after the fact—to smell him, which is so weird and out of character for her, being something she can't remember ever doing before to someone, and being something generally that she would think, were she to see someone else doing it, or if someone did it to her, would be really creepy, and so she falls back a few paces—he smells like tobacco and maybe cleaning solution and b.o., by the way, in a good way—and follows him through a dense stretch of forest where the snow is obscured by the canopy and the flakes that do manage to wrest through are meager and mostly disappear before they alight. They are going by her estimation due east. Soon there's a clear spacing between the trees and a rising in the ground and X Parke senses they're on a path—albeit blanketed in snow—which shrugs up onto a ridge and insinuates itself along the ridgeline while to the left the ground falls away until the ridgeline becomes an arête and below an expanse of snowy valley replete with glens and a cut of dark river and a buckling shape that at first X Parke confuses for an outcropping of boulder but which is most assuredly a structure, humungous there at the valley's nadir and like everything else swaddled in snow, and the boy now turning toward the arête's sheer edge and starting over, X Parke pausing to watch him trace his way down the 45°+ slope on mostly his butt using the heels of his orange sneakers to pickaxe the descent and crabwalking with his palms behind him, craning back to see if X Parke's following and seeing her not and shouting, "Just use the indentations from my shoes like stairs," and X Parke's hair convulsing in a sudden wind and shouting back, "What's your name even?" And here the boy looks at her like she's just said something completely outrageous and his eyes narrow and the skin creases around his eyes and a smile bleeds across his mouth and he laughs once at the low sky and says, "Malory. What's yours?"

"X Parke."

"The letter X?" still on his butt with his head craned all the way back so his face's upside down.

"Yeah."

"That's fantastic. The snow's worsening."

And here another gust really muscles X Parke toward the arête's edge and she reasons she'd rather go over by her own volition than the wind's and so sits and swings her legs over and starts extremely cursorily to slide after Malory who's already a good ways further along now, nearly halfway down the whole thing, X Parke's relatively very little Converse fitting easily inside the larger notches left by Malory's sneakers but still so nearly vertical she feels dangerously like she might just topple forward and plummet face-first to the cliff's base, wondering what she's doing all of a sudden here following this boy she doesn't know basically off a mountain, this boy who just happened to be wandering in the forest and happens to possess myriad qualities X Parke happens to find sort of devastatingly appealing. And then again she reconsiders that she, X Parke, also just happened to be wandering in the same forest and happens to possess at least some qualities, a sweater at least, probably more, that the boy finds appealing, and isn't it possible that he, the boy, Malory, is thinking the same thing about X Parke, namely how almost suspicious it is that she's out here like this, of all the people he could have run into, and so if they're both mutually suspicious and wondering what they're doing out here with the other and how this could have come to pass then that bodes well for there being no actual problem since the problem would be that if one of them was *not* suspicious and since X Parke *is* suspicious it stands to reason that Malory might be too though she can't know for sure. X Parke now navigating an especially sheer section of cliff, Malory 30ft below and dropping the remaining five feet to the bottom and shaking out his hair for some reason then squinting up at X Parke and displaying dual up-pointing thumbs and saying, "So close," to which X Parke starts to respond with something sarcastic but finds a thuck of hair in her mouth and spits it and jerks her head to clear the hair from her eyes, looks out briefly into the valley at the mammoth structure which, now so much closer, has acquired a daunting emanation wherein it really seems to rush toward X Parke who recoils and in doing so loses the grips of both hands and feet and slides down the cliff's face toward Malory's now outstretched arms, X Parke going "Fuckfuckfuckfuckfuck" and then squealing as her butt actually leaves the cliff and she does, as she feared, go forward face-first but only with six or seven feet to go and winds up somewhat actually gently collapsing into Malory's arms, Malory going "Oomph" and falling back and the two of them ending up in a sort of knot entwined there on the icy ground with the snow gathering down on them and obscuring their boundaries so from up here it's hard to say where one begins and the other one ends.

Malory then looking up at X Parke from beneath her, their faces very close, just by way of smiling and but his eyes crease and harden and his mouth spreads into a snarl and he goes, "My God, what's wrong with your *eye*?" X Parke here gasping and touching her eye, then the other eye, saying "What? *What?*" and Malory exhaling a brisk line of sweet tobacco-smelling breath into her face and sitting up a little so X Parke is now essentially on his lap, rubbing his own eyes and shaking his head. "Nothing I'm sorry," Malory saying, "Just a weird angle or something, for a second. An instant." But X Parke continuing to touch her eyes so Malory adding, "Your eye is fine. Both of them are fine. Better than fine, actually. You have wonderful normal eyes. I really like them."

X Parke looks away and tries not to smile, the two now helping each other up and starting along the valley's base toward the structure as the snow compounds. In high school X Parke'd had a friend, a boy but not a boyfriend, who she'd spent a good deal of time with in this one spot on the floor by some unused lockers in this dead end hall near the handicap bathroom with an oxidizing water fountain that was too close to the bathroom's door to reasonably drink from, the two of them sitting and sharing a set of earphones and listening to whatever, and this old non-boyfriend kind of reminds X Parke of this new boy Malory, not really in appearance but in some other way that X Parke can't quite lock down, having really to churn her feet through the shin-high snow now and realizing that Malory is holding her hand, or she's holding his, and is a little put off by how *not* uncomfortable this is and pretty certain she should probably be more uncomfortable but doing nothing to correct it, if that's the word, because not wanting to give Malory the impression that holding his hand is something she's uncomfortable with or that she thinks she should be uncomfortable with, now visoring her eyes from the snow with the other hand as the snow's gusted up straight into her face and Malory mutters something she's unable to make out, this old non-boyfriend having used to do pretty much the same thing while the two of them would sit on the floor outside the handicap bathroom reading or doodling or whatever and listening to music where the boy would say something under his breath that X Parke wouldn't catch, and she would look at him and say "Huh?" and even take out the earphone to expose her earhole, but the boy would merely shake his head and continue doodling or reading and X Parke would shrug and reinsert the earphone and ten or fifteen minutes later he would mutter something again and again X Parke would say "Huh?" or "What?" and remove the earphone and again the boy would shake his head and this would happen four-plus times a day while they sat there together usually during lunch or when skipping PE or during a free period and every time X Parke would say "Huh?" or "What?" even though she knew the boy wasn't going to reveal what he'd said and it kind of became a ritual or a habit for them and on reflection X Parke wonders if this didn't eventually constitute the majority of their communication over the years and then wonders where that boy might be now though there isn't anything she needs to say to him and she even realizes now as Malory starts to hurry toward the structure's perimeter where there's a dark configuration that might be steps and a door with X Parke wading through knee-deep snow with her eyes mostly down and really clasping Malory's hand that she doesn't even remember this high school boy's name.

Now here just as the wind does this scheming sort of laugh there's also hard floor underfoot and some tripping up steps, and door-sounds and X Parke's dragged forward by her hand and twirled and she helps facilitate the twirl and even giggles and there's sudden quiet warmth and subfusc light. "Phew," Malory says shaking out his hair again this time of snow, and X Parke does the same to hers and snowflakes spring out and tumble to the floor, the floor carpeted in this faded wall-to-wall carpet with beige flowers and bronze thorny vines and grayish deco blandishments and also numerous kidney-shaped water stains. "So. Welcome." Malory now gesturing melograndiosely, X Parke nodding around at the truly cavernous room whose walls yawn up into shadowy ceilings from which two—no three—enormous lightless brass chandeliers suspend like wraiths; salmon-colored floral wallpaper and dark wood wainscoting encircling the whole thing; X Parke breathing on her hands and turning in a circle; mealy curtains drawn shut along what must be very long windows at the room's southern length and bluish light transuding their edges; hallways branching from the room's perimeter everywhere X Parke looks and at the far end, through a doorless doorway, the ghostly resonance of a guttering flame. X Parke now following Malory toward that doorway, wiping her palms on her sweater and here alone with this boy indoors and following him further indoors and but maybe not as nervous about this as she should be. She tries to remember even the first letter of the non-boyfriend from high school's name and cannot. She tries to remember his face and also cannot. All she remembers is the shape of him beside her on the floor by the handicap bathroom and the umbilicus of earphones attaching them—and though now she also thinks he might've been in Ms. Inoue's Philosophy of Science elective with her. Is this the thing that's reminding her of him now? Not Malory but having been thinking about Ms. Inoue earlier and now encountering a boy, any boy, who is serving as a surrogate for the non-boyfriend boy in Ms. Inoue's elective? Malory disappears around the doorway's frame for a moment until X Parke catches up and there's another room, much smaller than the first but sizeable, at the far end of which's a fireplace in which's a gasp of flame; on the floor near the fireplace a nest of blankets and coverless pillows; beside the nest an arrangement of things: a plastic gallon of water for example and a tower of Pringles and a wilted bag of pretzels and some candy bars and a thick hardcover book spread in half pages-down; across the room a long window, curtainless, overlooking the bluing air and the valley and the silent raging snow, and beyond what must be a faint mountain's face cropped by the window's perimeter so there's only a plane of gauzy rock with no context. Malory goes to a semicircle of chairs arranged near the window and takes one and lifts it over his head and slams it onto the floor so it breaks into pieces. It makes a sound X Parke does not associate with a breaking chair, not a crack but a damp plop, like two uncorrelated phenomena that have been unjustly desegregated. Malory gathers up the chair's legs and feeds them into the fire carefully one at a time as if he's doing art. There's a smell X Parke's smelling now of mildew and stale water, standing just away from the floor's tangle of blankets with her fingers entwined at her waist and her Converse side-by-side nearly touching. Malory wipes his hands on the front of his jeans and takes off his Carhartt and casts it aside then sits on the nest of blankets with his knees drawn up and his forearms on his knees and stares into the fire like it's a TV or something, X Parke still behind him standing kind of very thinly, looking between Malory and the fire as snow beats against the long window. "What is this place?" X Parke asking now.

Malory gropes behind himself for the plastic gallon of water which is half-full or empty and locates it and takes a long drink from it in which two rivulets of water trickle from his lips' edges down his chin and drip into the baggy collar of his shirt, then sighs and wipes his mouth with a bare forearm and holds the gallon toward X Parke, who takes it tentatively. "I'm not sure, actually," he says. "I've only been here a week or so. I think it might've been a hotel but I haven't done a lot of exploring. The whole like north wing or whatever is burned, I think, like mostly burned down. It must've happened a long time ago since as you can see even this part is super decrepit. But that north wing is where all the rooms probably were, or that's at least what it looks like from the mouth of the hallway which is as far as I'm willing to go since the fire or whatever happened seems really to have degraded the structural integrity up there. Everything here in this south wing or whatever is like ballrooms and lobbies and stuff. This I think was a lounge or something. There's a kitchen through there, but nothing in it. As you can see I'm almost out of food, which is why I was out today when we ran into each other. I was scavenging I guess you could say. But what am I going to find in the middle of winter in the forest? It's not like I know how to like hunt or whatever. I'm going to have to figure something out soon. I'm almost out of cigarettes. And I ran out of booze this morning . . ." Here Malory swallows hard and cracks his neck.

X Parke meanwhile holding the plastic gallon with both hands and jutting out her lower jaw to pour a stream of water into her mouth without lip-contact, which she almost manages. "How'd you end up here, though, is my real question," she says.

Malory leans back onto the mound of blankets and entwines his fingers behind his head. "It's kind of . . . it's a long story and stuff. I'll tell you but then you have to tell me stuff about you too."

X Parke now crouches beside the blankets. "Fine."

Malory closes his eyes and breathes deeply thrice, then opens them and they explode with firelight. "I kind of ran away from rehab back in September. Actually not so much 'ran away' as just left and didn't go home. My family lives in the city and I was waiting for a bus back there and then I saw this kid, this little kid at the bus stop with his mom, and the kid looked, I thought at least, exactly like me. Just a littler version of me. And he was standing with his mom who looked just like my mom and who was talking to this guy, some guy with a ponytail who was also waiting for the bus and you could tell they weren't together, like they hadn't showed up together and you could just tell by the way they were talking, the mom and this guy, like they were talking like strangers who wanted to *not* be strangers, if that makes sense. Anyway this kid was there standing by his mom and looking exactly like me and for whatever reason I felt like I should just be friendly or something or comment on the resemblance between me and this kid so I approached them and said 'Excuse me, sorry, I just wanted to say that your son looks pretty much exactly like I looked when I was a kid.' And the kid and the mom kind of just blink at me as if I hadn't said real words and the man with the ponytail smiles this like very amused and cocky smile and sort of rolls his hand which has these crazy old tattoos on it and says 'Is this how it sees itself?' just like that with those pronouns. 'Is this how it sees itself.' And all I could do was back away and go stand on the other side of the bus stop and smoke and I kept looking back at the boy and his mom and the more I looked at them the more I started to realize that the boy didn't look like me as much as I thought, and the mom didn't look like my mom really at all, and I started to feel really ashamed and confused and meanwhile across the street from the bus stop was a liquor store and every time I looked back over at the boy he looked less like I thought he did, and like as he became more dissimilar the liquor store became more inviting until I was just on my way across the street and I bought a fifth of Jack and walked a ways until I found a park and I sat and drank for the first time in . . . in months."

X Parke looks around the room which is darkening now as the light outside hardens into navy and the snow can no longer be seen. "I don't know what to say."

Malory exhales briskly through his nose. "Anyway since then I've kind of just been zigzagging around. I have no money, really, so mostly I've been staying in places like this, or in people's unoccupied summer homes and stuff, or just wherever I can find a bed or," he looks down, "a floor."

"And drinking."

"Yeah and drinking. Until now. I don't know what I'm going to do."

X Parke extends her legs toward the fireplace. "I wish I knew how to help you."

"Honestly, just some company is helpful. I didn't realize how lonely I was. And of all the people who could've just magically showed up in the woods, you're like the best possible one."

X Parke allowing her hair to curtain her face. "Why's that?"

"Cause you're just cool. I mean, you and I are, like, we're obviously kindred spirits. I think we're like probably already best friends."

The fire crepitates, a hand of embers opening and winking up the flue. X Parke's and Malory's legs are parallel to each other, X Parke's of course much shorter so her Converse going only to around Malory's shins, and they are both sitting with their palms on the floor behind them for support and though they are not touching X Parke can sense Malory's skin close to her's and the closeness whets her pulse.

"Anyway, your turn," Malory opens the tower of Pringles and screws a beak of fingers inside. "Where were you on your way from before your plane crashed?"

"College."

"So you were just going home to see your family for winter break or something?"

"Yes and no. Yes it's winter break and so I was going home to see them because I have the time, but no that's not the only reason."

"Why else?"

"I don't want you to think there's something wrong with me."

A smile gashes Malory's face apart. "Can I kiss you again?"

"Did we already start kissing?"

"No, actually."

"Let's wait then."

"Okay. But tell me."

"It's that I realized something kind of frightening a few months ago and I need to talk to my family about it. I realized . . ."

"What did—sorry."

"I realized that I can't remember anything from before I was twelve or thirteen. Nothing. It's just, like, empty space no stars. And then my first memory is of being scared in bed and not being able to see over the foot of the bed and thinking there's something there or not there I don't know. And so I'm just worried about the implications. Like I've heard things about that, about what might cause that, and I know it's not normal because when I realized it, when I discovered the memory problem, I was playing this game with my friends Jessa and Jessa and they were just rattling things off from their whole lives, things from their childhoods that they just knew and could talk about as if they'd happened yesterday, and I was sitting there realizing that I couldn't do that at all, that there was nothing. And I guess maybe the craziest part or most concerning part is that before I played that stupid game with the Jessas I didn't have any idea that the entire first two-thirds of my life were missing, like it never crossed my mind, and then as soon as I did realize it it became the biggest thing in my life and was distracting me from everything and making me stressed and making me act in really weird and inappropriate ways sometimes. Like with this one professor of mine who I had a little crush on which wasn't a big deal but because I wasn't really thinking about anything except this memory problem I was therefore distracted and not paying attention to how I was acting and I think I really embarrassed myself a few times just by acting weird around him which wouldn't be the first time I've acted weird around a teacher because there was this other teacher in high school, Ms. Inoue, who I really liked and who was a really good dresser and back then of course I wasn't aware of the memory problem but still managed to act weird around her when I was meeting with her after class in the little conference room in the back of the library and she was sitting next to me showing me something in a book, I don't remember what, and she was wearing this green almost felty dress she always wore and just randomly that day the slit in the side of it was open along her thigh which was near me under the table and there was a rent in her stocking along the thigh where I could see her bare skin and I was looking down at it while she was talking and for some completely insane reason and like completely outside of my volition I reached down and traced the strip of bare skin with my finger and Ms. Inoue stops talking and looks at me just completely startled—and who can blame her—and then she pulls the dress's slit closed over her leg and resumes showing me whatever she was showing me only at that point we were both distracted, me by my mortification at having done what I'd done and her at *her* mortification at what I'd done and we never talked about it. And that was the same day I remember all of a sudden right now that a bird managed to get trapped in the library and me and Ms. Inoue watched it bash its head apart on the bookshelves and then die somewhere high up and I don't know if they ever got its body out. And anyway that was off-topic and just an example of the ways that I was weird even before I discovered the memory problem and now especially with the memory problem I just feel weird and wrong. And I need to talk to my family about it."

Malory nodding gravely in the fire's light, the Pringles can dangling from his hand. "I have a similar thing. My earliest memory is of looking out through a window at a long lawn that sloped downward away from me toward a lake, or a pond maybe, and the lawn starting to roll, or undulate, in waves toward the house, the house I was looking out from. And I remember my mom holding me up to the window to watch, and other relatives were there, and they were all smiling and oohing and aahing at the giant ripples in the lawn but in a way that underneath I could tell they were afraid, and that they were feigning amusement for my benefit, since I was basically just a baby, and they didn't want me to be scared of whatever was happening. And but the thing was is that I don't think I knew inherently that there was anything scary about the undulating lawn itself, because I was too little, but I *did* know that the way my relatives were behaving was off. Like they were smiling and speaking in these kinds of lilting voices but the muscles around their eyes were taut and their hands were all knuckled up and I knew that something wasn't right because of that, because of the fear that was leaking out of them, and that's what scared me so bad that I started to cry . . . even though I don't actually remember crying, I just remember my vision kind of wilting and everything getting dingy and then being carried from the room. And I assume that was me crying because what else could it have been? Though the weird thing is that I've brought this memory up to my family—namely my mom but also certain other relatives who I could have sworn were there—and no one has any idea what

I'm talking about. They all claim that if something like that had actually happened that they would absolutely remember it, which of course they would. But it's so incredibly vivid in my mind and for most of my life I've walked around thinking it was my earliest memory, like the moment when my brain sort of clicked on, and it was totally formative and integral and anyway at this point I'm pretty much convinced that I either dreamed it or inherited it from somewhere else, or someone else, and kind of accepting that has really skewed my whole idea about myself and made me question other memories or even other things entirely, like just ideas about life and stuff . . ." Malory looking at X Parke as if for the first time and then squinching his eyes and gritting his teeth and placing the point of his index to his temple and cocking his thumb. "Sorry I didn't mean to just make that about myself. Something I'm working on. What do you study at college?"

"Well I'm a first semester freshman so I haven't picked a major yet but I'm on a humanities track right now. I think I'm going to major in literature."

"What do you like to read?"

"I think Gardiner Blythe is my favorite writer. I had a great professor this year who really helped me start to get my head around it, and now I feel like, you know, I don't know. Have you read him?"

Malory's astounding blue eyes spiral toward X Parke. "Are you . . ." He leans aside and drags the hardcover book toward him and lifts it and displays it for X Parke. There's this moment now where

X Parke clocks the book and its title and then looks sort of around it toward the fireplace where the fire shivers and snaps and she thinks there's something wrong here and she needs to get out.

"I don't believe it," Malory's saying, moving the book to block X Parke's view of the fire. "Of all the fucking authors in the world, you just mention Gardiner Blythe right now? I don't believe it. I genuinely don't believe you're real."

X Parke reaches out and takes the hardcover copy of *The Long Pig* and sets it on her lap. The room's long window is dark now and reflects or refracts only the pale orange aura of the fire.

"I started reading it in rehab and I'm basically obsessed now," Malory saying. "I haven't read anything else by him and this is kind of a drastic introduction. Some of it I feel like I don't understand."

"It helps to sort of divide sections up into dueling concepts, like DEATH and SEX or LIMINAL and ABSOLUTE. There're these sort of columns you can draw to help organize the ideas in the book. I don't know . . ."

"Will you read to me?"

X Parke having to sit forward off her hands because her wrists are stiffening. "It's a little dark."

"We'll move, come here." Malory drags the blankets nearer to the fireplace.

"Where do you want me to read from?"

"From where it's open."

X Parke traces the page's edge with a thumb's nail, the beginning of Chapter 5. Chapter 5 is one she'd spent two weeks on in class with Professor Lane, it being especially tricky to work out how it's doing what it's doing or even what it's doing at all. Chapter 5 had kept getting in her way, too, when she was writing her final essay, and was one of the reasons she was almost late getting the paper in. Because no matter how she'd crafted her thesis statement there was always something in Chapter 5 and Chapter 5 alone that got in the way of it and undid it. An unruly and contrarian chapter. X Parke almost wonders if Blythe hadn't written it specifically and sadistically for the purposes of obfuscating analysis. Pretty much the whole thing is a monologue from an ultimately peripheral character, and its influence on the larger text seemed even to stump Prof Lane who at a point during one of the classes set aside for the chapter stood at the chalkboard and drew his columns and then dangled the chalk there for a solid minute before replacing it on the board's ledge and returning to the lectern and asking the class for suggestions on how to categorize a useful duality in this case. X Parke doesn't remember what, if anything, was decided upon. Now she takes a few deep breaths as Malory smoothes a section of blankets beside him and gestures, rummages through his pockets and comes up with a rumpled pack of cigarettes from which he digs one and sets it in his teeth and leans his head into the fireplace to light. He exhales dark clouds which obscure his face and lies on his side with one hand propped under his head and looks at X Parke, his eyes and face shadowish with the fire behind him, X Parke sitting on her knees and holding the book flat on her lap or canted slightly forward to catch the fire's light and beginning to read, her voice and the cigarette's smoke and the fire's smoke emulsifying and the room seeming to shrink or tighten so the space between her and Malory lessens and the fire is huge and X Parke reads but her eyes are fixed on a dark pit in the blankets where her and Malory's hands are together, not touching but occupying the same space, one inside the other, and it feels like nothing.

PART II

A Whole Nother Thing

5

Later: the fire in embers: their bodies dilute the blankets and Malory's speaking in the privacy of the dark.

". . . I explained all this to my counselor at the Chavanuck Valley Center for Addiction Treatment the first time we met, which I think caught him off guard since he probably isn't used to people just spilling their guts like that the first day they get to rehab. But he was cool about it and he listened and when I was done he sort of shrugged and shook his head, like the significance of the story was too great to fathom. And then he started to ask something but stopped and told me to head back to the common room. And on my way to the main building I tried to speculate about what he might have been about to ask me and kind of settled on something like 'Why on earth are you telling me this?' and I felt embarrassed about being too forthcoming or something, and I imagined shooting myself in the head with my fingers except they shot real bullets and the side of my head came off and my brain fell out.

"Anyway I tried to make a point moving forward of not over-sharing to my counselor during our sessions—or at least not sharing things that he didn't, you know, ask me specifically to share. And I did a pretty good job of it for the most part. In fact there may have even been a session or three where I was downright remote. Interestingly these were the sessions that I walked out feeling most fulfilled, which I guess is a little counterintuitive seeing as these were the sessions where, in my mind, the least actual therapy had occurred, at least insofar as I'd always thought of therapy as being, which was as a kind of dialogue wherein the therapist coaxed the therapee to vocalize as frankly and unpremeditatedly as possible their thoughts and feelings and in the process sort of stumble onto a kind of truth about their self that came as a disclosure and a surprise to them, that revealed something they knew about their self that they were either too afraid to admit or acknowledge or didn't sort of consciously realize until they talked their self into a corner and heard their self say it aloud. In that way I had always thought of therapy as a kind of auto-gotcha journalism. Though to be clear I knew very little about therapy before arriving at CVCAT, having spent pretty much my entire life up until then being drunk and high, and why exactly I thought it reasonable to take any position on about what did or did not constitute therapy spoke volumes about my mindset.

"And this place of just feeling wrong or misconceived dominated my early rehab experience. It felt in a lot of ways like I was seeing the world somewhat aslant, or like three paces back from my own face, where information was being garbled on its way to my brain so that even if I knew what to do with it when it arrived it was unreliable source material. Now I can't say for certain that this sensation was *new* to me then, since as I've mentioned I was just generally fucked up for so long that I can't comment with any authority on my prior state of mind. But I can say that it was the first time I noticed it. And it caused a great deal of discomfort. For example the first time I saw RN Simone, who was this really very extremely beautiful and zaftig and vaguely Mediterranean or Middle Eastern-looking lady who worked at CVCAT and who couldn't have been too much older than me—in fact she may have been younger, since I kept forgetting I'm in my deep twenties and was just arrested in this place of feeling nineteen or whatever and so was always caught off guard by thinking people were older than me when they weren't—who the first time I saw her at the med window my second or third night at CVCAT smiled at me so sweetly and alluringly and her hair was just thick and black and fighting to explode out of its little tortoiseshell hairclip, that I became convinced in that instant that she was completely in love with me and that I could very readily be that completely in love with her too. Later that same night, when I was sitting and smoking in the smoking gazebo and all the other guys—who I barely knew at that point because I'd pretty much just gotten down there—were joking around and stuff, one of them brought up RN Simone and started saying some pretty disrespectful stuff about her, like about all the stuff he wanted to do to her, and the other guys joined in and tried to one-up each other with the, like, super-aggressive pornographic stuff they would do to RN Simone given the opportunity, and I found myself growing annoyed, and then frustrated, and then just outright pissed, and I started rehearsing in my head something to say about it, like this whole speech about how objectifying women is dangerous for men too, and is part of the mindset that turned us into addicts in the first place, and that if you stop and think about it, RN Simone is here to help us, has chosen to do this with her life over all the other arguably easier or more lucrative things she could have done, and that we should be grateful and express our gratitude by showing her some respect. But then before I could open my mouth RN Simone herself walked up in her turquoise scrubs and all the guys got quiet and a few of them giggled and she told us it was time to go inside and that lights-out was in fifteen minutes. And that time, when she was there at the smoking gazebo, she didn't look at me at all—in fact I thought I noticed her looking especially much at a couple of the *other* guys—and I started to question whether the smile she'd given me earlier had been what I'd thought it had been, or if it had happened at all.

"Then like a week later I was sitting on my bed reading *The Long Pig*, which I'd found lying around, and I read that first chapter about, you know, that planet orbiting through the nether regions of our solar system, just *phew*, and I was sitting there kind of imagining that there actually could be this distant, gelid monster kind of lurking through the dark . . . and anyway Terry, my roommate—a nice guy, a general practitioner—was sitting on his bed across from me, just kind of staring off as if into the bowels of space, and maybe twenty minutes went by like that, with me reading and occasionally glancing up at Terry and him just staring past me. Then finally all of a sudden Terry went: 'Am I sleeping?' like that with his eyes open, and I said: 'No, Terry, I don't think so.' And Terry kind of straightened up and blinked around with this confused expression, like he'd never seen anything in the world before, and eventually his eyes settled on me and he started to nod and I said: 'What's up? Are you okay?' and he said: 'I just had the weirdest dream—and I hope you don't take it the wrong way—but I just dreamed that I was sitting here on my bed watching you and RN Simone have sex on your bed . . .' And I scoffed and shrugged and then said: 'Man, I wouldn't mind having that dream,' and Terry said: 'I don't know what it means, though.' And I pretended to read, though really I was thinking about Terry's dream, and why he might have had it, and if it meant that he thought something about me and RN Simone or if it just meant that he was a horny old doctor and I happened to be in the wrong place at the wrong time while he had a sex-dream about a hot nurse.

"Now I need to mention something about Terry, namely what ended up happening to him, which is that a week after his dream about me and RN Simone, I found him in our room slumped on his side at the foot of his bed in this very odd position where his arms were sticking out behind him kind of unnaturally straight, like locked in this rigid place, and his fingers were gnarled around one another like a thuck of branches or bramble, and though I couldn't see his face behind his nest of black hair, I feared it might be contorted into a horrible grimace or, like, listing to one side the way that happens with stroke victims or whatever. Though he hadn't had a stroke I learned later, and his face—when I rushed to him and looked—was actually really peaceful, almost in a way that made me feel sort of nostalgic or something, or envious of just how much *serenity* he seemed to have in that moment. And anyway I did all the right things, meaning I ran out and got a staff member who called an ambulance and later I learned that Terry had managed to sneak some benzos onto the premises and had swallowed a palm-full and basically OD'd and a few days later we heard he'd discharged himself from the hospital and was AWOL and I guess if anything good came out of it it was that all of a sudden I had the entire room to myself.

"Which coincidentally was the same time that RN Simone took a shift change and started doing PM room-checks, which is when they go around and make sure everyone is in bed with the lights out or at least in bed reading or whatever. And so pretty much the same day Terry left I started getting nighttime visits from RN Simone. The first time it surprised me, like I was lying there reading and the door opened and I half-glanced over expecting to see one of the usual RNs, but there was RN Simone in her turquoise scrubs with her hair just wrestling out of its clip, and my heart stuttered and I probably blushed or something because I was in my underwear on top of the sheets, and her eyes kind of skittered and her fingers sort of pattered along the doorframe, and she stepped into the room a little but then stepped back out and just said: 'Everything good?' And I put the book down over my lap and nodded and said: 'Yeah . . . How are you?' And she just nodded and then this moment kind of unfurled where she just stood there looking at me and I was looking back at her and then finally she said: 'Goodnight,' and shut the door pretty abruptly in a way that made it seem like maybe it meant something and a minute later I had to masturbate because she had been so close to my bed and my naked skin that I could almost feel the, like, cool yieldingness of her scrubs on me and I imagined just pulling those scrubs down over and over—and the thought of her coming back in and catching me was just insanely enticing and so I kept prolonging it, like not allowing myself to finish, just kind of hoping—and fearing—she would walk back in. Though after maybe thirty minutes, when she didn't reappear, I couldn't take it anymore and so finally let myself cum but it was the weirdest thing, because after, when I looked down, there was no semen or anything, though I'd felt it come out, and I sort of turned this over in my head, like why this might have happened, and for some reason I was pretty sure it had happened before, like a long time ago . . . though I might have been remembering something else. And anyway a little while later I masturbated again and that time everything happened the way it was supposed to and so I dismissed the whole thing as just a misunderstanding, the way people do sometimes with things like that.

"And so from then on, every night, I began paying really close attention to how I was positioned in the bed, like almost maybe a little obsessively. Like I would stack the pillows so that I was at this very particular angle that I thought made my abs sort of flex nicely, and I would bunch the sheets very strategically around my crotch to accentuate that whole part, and I always made sure I was clean, that my teeth were brushed, my nails cut, etc, in case RN Simone ever came in further than the doorway. And every night, always either earlier or later than I expected, the door would open and there she would be, her hair just this rambunctious black surge, and she would look in at me and deliver any of a range of expressions: sometimes a smile; sometimes a kind of curious look as if I was doing something unusual; sometimes this squint, like she was trying to see me better; and once or twice barely a glance, barely anything but the click of a knob, a flash of turquoise and black hair, another click. On these occasions I would spend the rest of the night shooting myself in the head over and over until there was no head left.

"The days went by the way they do. It occurred to me that rehab was designed to deaden the passage of time. Like each day was arranged to imitate the day before so that after awhile you started to forget there was any other way to live. After about a month and a half I no longer thought at all about things on the outside, about, like, the wreckage of my life. I sort of fixated on completing the recursive tasks of the day and became immersed in the small, hermetic land inside the CVCAT property. And I started to realize something about how a person's sense of themselves is determined by their environment. Like for example: day in and day out I would just see the same guys, the same group of twenty guys or whatever, and I started to—and I mean, this is awkward to say but it's true—I started to find myself inadvertently thinking about some of them. And to be clear, it's not like I'm this rigid or raging heterosexual, but I am heterosexual, and but just being surrounded by really mostly men, like 99% men all the time, had this effect where I guess my mind sort of created a recourse for all the pent up sexual frustration I was feeling. Like I started to channel some of that into just whoever was in my, like, immediate vicinity. And it made me wonder if this was how a person's sexuality sort of formed in general, like just by whatever the predominance of other people was like, whatever was available during the sort of formative period of a person's life. And it wasn't anything explicit, it's just that occasionally I found my mind wandering . . . Like when I would masturbate at night thinking about RN Simone I would sometimes have these thoughts creep in about maybe one or two of the guys watching me masturbate while thinking about her, or even me watching one or two of *them* masturbate while thinking about her. And anyway it wasn't troubling or concerning or anything, because I understood that sexuality and stuff was a continuum or whatever, but it was just that it was new, I think . . . though as I mentioned before I couldn't be sure since my memory was hazy about so much that came before this.

"And in retrospect I don't know what I was thinking but I ended up mentioning this to my counselor during one of our sessions, just about how I was kind of noticing my thoughts wandering to new places, and in particular to these sorts of sexual places about some of the other guys at CVCAT. And while I spoke my counselor sat very still with his legs crossed—which was awkward for him because he was heavy—and looked out from his mess of dark hair toward the base of my chair, and I could sense his discomfort or almost hear his thoughts, which were, like: 'Please stop telling me this. I don't want to hear it. Why are you telling me this? Please stop.' And as I spoke I started to feel incredibly embarrassed and emasculated and realized I needed to change the topic and so pivoted away without really paying attention to what I had pivoted to until it was too late and I'd already blurted out that I thought RN Simone might have a crush on me. And then I kept going and said that I didn't want to get her in trouble or anything, I just thought I should say something because to be honest all the attention she was giving me was distracting me from the work I was supposed to be doing on myself. And at this point my counselor looked up at me, just looked at me out of his face with one of his knuckles wedged against his lips so that the lip skin sort of bunched up under his nose, and he said: 'I want to address something with you that your father mentioned last time he and I talked. Something that happened last winter, I think, involving a girlfriend of yours . . . Do you know what I'm referring to?' And here I kind of waited a few seconds and scrunched up my eyes to imply that maybe I didn't immediately know what he was talking about, then said: 'I think so, yeah. But it wasn't my fault. It was a misunderstanding.' And my counselor nodded and turned up his palms as if to show that he of course believed me and that this belief should go without saying, and then he said: 'So tell me what happened as it happened in real life . . .' So I told him the story about how last winter I was visiting my dad and stepmom at their place in the city to see their new baby—who was under a year old at that point—and I brought this girl I was dating, Dana, who really, looking back, was nothing more than a fuck/drinking buddy and had no business meeting my family. But I brought her over and everyone was very cordial and we were all just hanging out in the living room chatting and Dana was on the floor playing with the baby, holding it under the arms and making faces at it and stuff and the baby was sort of smiling its chubby cheeks and looking around just taking in the world which I could only imagine was just this awesome roaring blur to it. And anyway I was chatting with my dad and stepmom and at one point I kind of looked down at Dana and the baby right as Dana just, like, *shook* it really hard, so that its head snapped back on its little neck and its eyes kind of crossed and then blinked around completely stunned. And I looked at my dad and my stepmom but they were looking off in the other direction, talking about some piece of furniture they didn't like or whatever, and then Dana did it again—just jerked the shit out of the baby—and again my dad and stepmom didn't see it and I could tell that Dana was about to do it *again* because her arms tensed up and her bottom lip kind of tucked under her teeth and her wild black hair sort of bristled, and I had to do something to stop her. I had to do something. . . .

"'So you kicked her in the face,' said my counselor.

"'Just enough to, like, stun her. So I could grab the baby away.'

"'Your father claims that no one saw her shaking the baby.'

"'Yeah they weren't looking.'

"'Why do you think she would have done that?'

"'I don't know . . .' I looked down at the floor, at the base of my counselor's chair. Talking about all this I could almost hear the baby's sort of rending shrieks and see my dad's and stepmom's shocked faces, the blood leaking out of Dana's nose. I could taste the coppery dryness of my own mouth. 'Maybe, I don't know, like reliving something? Maybe someone shook her when *she* was a baby?'

"My counselor sniffed, uncrossed and recrossed his legs. 'Maybe,' he said. Then he started to say something else but stopped and instead went: 'You have group in a few minutes. We can talk more about this next time we meet.'

"'Or not,' I said, standing. 'Or we can never talk about it again.'

"'Or we can never talk about it again.'

"And so of course I ended up thinking about this for the rest of the day, kind of mulling it over, trying to figure out why my counselor had brought it up when he did and what he might be trying to tell me. I paced around the property, eventually ending up sitting in the back of the common room while a few guys watched TV. The show they were watching was one I'd never seen, with actors I didn't recognize all involved in a premise I couldn't follow. Intermittently the guys would laugh at something that happened, and so for a minute I tried to make an effort to pay attention, to see what was so funny. A group of characters sat around in an apartment, just sitting there not talking or anything, and then gradually this sound, like a cat mewling, started from off-screen. At first the mewling was normal, just like the sound a cat makes when it's hungry or cranky or whatever, but then it started to, like, elevate, to grow louder and more violent, to kind of morph into a more sort of guttural and pained noise, until eventually it was no longer clear that it even *was* a cat mewling instead of, like, an adult human in some kind of horrendous pain. And the characters on-screen just blinked around at each other really awkwardly, or very kind of deliberately avoided eye contact in a blatant way, and here the guys watching the show laughed, and again I couldn't figure out what was funny and in fact found the whole thing decidedly *not* funny but rather sort of quite disturbing. Then one of the characters said what sounded to me like: 'Bingo. Grave digging answers for itself,' at which point the guys in the common room laughed again pretty uproariously. And I brought my shoulders up to my ears and delivered what I imagined was a sharply incredulous look to the empty back of the common room and when I looked back toward the TV I saw all the guys looking at me and realized I must have inadvertently made a sound or something to draw attention to myself and I felt my face get hot and went: 'I don't get it . . .' but said it way too quietly so that not even I could hear it with my own ears only inches from my mouth and so therefore there was no way the guys could hear it almost, like, fifteen or more feet across the room. And they all exchanged looks with one another and I was too embarrassed to just flee even though that was so badly what I wanted to do and so instead I just sat there and shot myself in the head until the guys all became preoccupied again with the show and then I tried to sneak out of the room though when I glanced back from the doorway I saw one of the guys watching me through the bangs of his black hair with this, like, knowing sort of smirk or something on his face and as I made my way across the property back toward my room I had this feeling like I was forgetting something of extreme importance though of course it was just a feeling and didn't apply to anything concrete in my life.

"That night happened to be one of the two nights a week that we were allowed to make phone calls. What they did is they would bring in a landline to each unit, plug it into the phone jack there, and then you would have zero privacy to make your call while the other guys in your unit stood there and waited their turns. I had forewent making calls so far after seeing the way that some of the other guys became extremely stressed out while talking to their wives and girlfriends and families, since more often than not those conversations devolved into arguments or whatever and left the guys feeling frustrated and trapped and paranoid. But that night I felt this, like, suffocating claustrophobia, like this sense that the boundaries of CVCAT had been readjusted to encompass the whole world, and I felt a need to reach outside, to sort of undergird my knowledge that of course the rest of the world still existed. So I took a turn with the phone and but then kind of stood there trying to figure out who, exactly, to call. My options were limited, because I only had three numbers memorized, those being each of my parents' numbers and my own, and my dad, I think, felt a little, like, somehow contaminated to me by the conversation I'd had earlier with my counselor. So I called my mom, and as it rang I tried to come up with something to say, accounting for both the fact that she and I hadn't spoken since I was despondent in the psych-ward *and* for the audience of guys currently waiting nearby. But the phone just rang and rang, and I realized she wasn't going to answer, and so instead of planning or rehearsing what to say I wondered about *why* she wasn't answering, like if she was deliberately ignoring me and if this meant something for the future of our relationship, and how could I have possibly fucked things up so bad that my own mother couldn't even bear to hear my voice? But then, after maybe ten rings, she picked up, and her voice sounded far away, and she said: 'Hello,' just flat like that, like totally emotionless. And her voice, like the register of it and its pitch and whatever, sounded different than it existed in my memory, and I genuinely worried I'd dialed the wrong number and so I said: 'Mom?' and she said: 'Yes.' And so I tried to picture her and said: 'How are you?' And she said: 'Fine,' just in the same flat way. And then I waited a few seconds for her to ask me how I was doing, but she didn't, and so I said: 'Things are okay here, for the most part . . .' and as I said it I realized that I was, like, performing for the guys who were standing around me waiting to use the phone, like feigning a healthy, normal conversation with my mom so that they couldn't know how unhealthy and abnormal our relationship was. And I heard her sigh through the phone and then she said: 'Good. I'm glad to hear that.' And I said 'Yeah . . .' and then waited again for what felt like forever, and at one point just started nodding as if she was speaking, and then out of nowhere, like completely just by surprise, I heard myself say: 'I want to come home.' And there was silence on the other end and I rubbed my face and sort of knotted the phone chord around my wrist and then right when I thought she'd hung up or something she said: 'Well you can't right now . . . And besides, there was a . . . an earthquake here.' And I thought I'd misheard her and said: 'Sorry?' and she said: 'There was an earthquake here a few days ago.' And I'd never heard of an earthquake in the city and so I said: 'You're kidding,' and she said: 'No. Not kidding. A big hole—a fissure, they're calling it—opened up on the street.' And this time she sounded more like I remembered her sounding and I said: 'Is everybody okay?' And she said: 'Yes, no one was hurt. And the apartment seems fine for now. They're coming next week to pour concrete into the . . . into the *fissure*.' And I said: 'Wow. That's truly insane . . .' And then there was just another long silence during which I heard her sigh two or three times and finally I said: 'Well listen, some of the other guys are waiting to use the phone, so I'm gonna go . . .' And she said: 'Alright,' and then I said: 'I love you,' and she said, flatly: 'I love you, too.' And then she hung up and I put the phone down and got out of the way for the next guy and ended up wandering out to the smoking gazebo and sitting with the guys there and kept wanting to mention to them that there was an earthquake and a fissure but everyone was talking to someone else and I never got the chance.

"And then as the evening progressed I started to get this feeling that the person I'd spoken to on the phone hadn't actually been my mom at all but just someone who sounded enough like her that I'd kind of, like, tricked myself into thinking it was her. Because the truth was is that the odds were not completely miniscule that I'd dialed the wrong number and called someone else's mom by mistake. And I tried to replay the conversation looking for some indication that it had to have been my mom and not someone else's, like something she'd said that I could use as undeniable proof that it was actually her. And the closest I could find was the exchange about me wanting to come home and her saying I couldn't, though reasonably that could have been relevant to a range of contexts besides my own. And the more I thought about it the more it started to seem that the voice I'd spoken to on the phone had *not* been the voice of my mom, but someone else's voice without even that great a similarity, like just a completely different voice. And suddenly I felt this kind of explosive urge to call my *actual* mom, to hear her real voice and have a true conversation and erase this, like, dirtiness I felt from being confused—though of course by then they'd already removed the phones from the units and wouldn't bring them back for days.

"And I think because of this I was preoccupied or distracted or whatever later while in bed, and I pretty much forgot or lapsed or something on the fact that RN Simone was going to appear, and so I didn't attend to any of my usual preparations. Like instead of arranging myself strategically I was just basically sprawled on the bed fully dressed with my book closed in my hand, staring at the ceiling and thinking about the voice I'd spoken to on the phone which the more I thought about it the kind of deeper and cracklier it became in my head, until it was just, like, downright demonic. And when my door opened and RN Simone appeared I was genuinely surprised—I actually flinched, believe it or not—and then I was even *more* surprised when she just stepped into the room and closed the door behind her and then stood there leaning against it, looking at me, with strands of her black hair kind of reaching out in every direction as if for balance, and the collar of her turquoise scrubs sort of twisted off to the side, and for a long moment we just looked at each other—her with this look as if she was about to either explode into laughter or collapse into tears—and me with whatever look my face had when there were absolutely no thoughts in my head.

"'I'm sorry . . .' she said finally, hanging her head. I sat up and turned toward her and said: 'Are you okay?' And she nodded and then shook her head and said: 'This job can be stressful.' And I said: 'What happened?' And she took a breath and pushed a clump of black hair from her face and said: 'Nothing . . . I'm so sorry. This is so inappropriate . . .' And I started to stand, like, compelled all of a sudden to go to her. But I stopped myself, and I said: 'No, no. It's okay . . .' And she said: 'I just feel like . . . you're not like these other guys.' And hearing her say this I felt my heart swell or whatever, and I said: 'In what ways?' And she sniffled and wiped her face with the back of her hand and said: 'I'm sorry . . . This is wrong,' and then just turned and left the room and left me sitting there in the sort of reverberating aftermath, struggling to decide if she had even been there at all. But then I heard the door to the unit open and close, and I spread the blinds and watched her through the window beside my bed as she hurried down the path, and I could barely see her in the dark, and the shadows in the grass alongside her seemed to gutter around her legs, and curl up her back and rummage through her hair and oppress her and, finally, swallow her whole.

"The next morning I saw her at the med window, and she seemed to have a hard time looking at me which I found really endearing and which emboldened me to speak: 'Have you even been home since last night?' 'Briefly,' she said, and I asked: 'Are you here all day again?' And she said: 'Yeah,' and handed me a plastic cup filled with my meds and I became, like, painfully aware in that moment of what a heaping pile of medicine I had to take—for my *brain* of all things, no less—and felt myself blush. And I glanced around to make sure there was no one listening and then said: 'You know, if you ever need to talk . . .' But she had turned around as I said it, to put my med case back in its locker, and I didn't know if she'd heard me, and I kind of scurried away and headed to my AM group, and felt sort of halfway between giddy—at the prospect of a special connection blooming between me and RN Simone—and this almost curdling humiliation that I really couldn't place.

"And group felt especially cutting that day for some reason, like one of the guys really spilled his shit to us about how when he was a child his mom used to come into his room at night and stand over his bed and scream at him. And not, like, words or anything, but also not just regular screaming, but this kind of gibberish, like this seething kind of nonsense that the guy claimed he still heard sometimes, even now—*especially* now that he was getting sober. And it was so weird because obviously that was what had happened to *that* guy, that was *his* Bad Stuff, but for some reason it felt so familiar to me, and I started to think that, like, maybe it was possible that I'd experienced the same Bad Stuff and even started to have memories of it somehow, like memories of my own mom poised over my bed, her unruly black hair draped around me, her wide body blotting the doorway . . . and her voice, steaming, hissing, crashing over everything . . . But it didn't make sense, because I hadn't had those memories before hearing this guy tell his story, and so obviously I was inventing them or whatever, though they were so vivid, and anyway after group ended I went up to that guy and told him just how grateful I was to him for sharing that stuff, because it had opened some things up for me. And he gave me this sort of quizzical look, as if whatever I'd said hadn't made any sense on some level, but then he shrugged and said: 'That's cool, I'm glad,' and then walked ahead to talk to some other guys, and I tried to figure out which part of what I'd said hadn't made sense, like if it had been a contextual issue, or a grammatical one, or if I'd just somehow made sounds that weren't words, or if he'd simply misheard me.

"Then that afternoon, right after lunch while I was standing at the gazebo smoking, I saw my counselor kind of waddling up the path from the main building, coming directly toward me. It was hot, and the sun was especially bared, and by the time he arrived he was sweating and a little out of breath and his curly black hair was matted across his forehead. 'I need to talk to you,' he said, gesturing at me. A couple of the other guys shot each other looks, and one of them went: 'Uh oh!' and there was some laughter, and I shrugged and forced a grin and followed my counselor back along the path. Though we didn't make it all the way to the main building because he veered off at one point into a patch of shade beneath a tree and turned to face me with his upper lip tucked under his teeth. And right before I asked him what was going on he said: 'Your father called.' And I said: 'Okay.' And he said: 'We spoke for awhile about whether or not to tell you this, given where you are and how important it is not to get distracted . . .' And I said: '. . . And?' And he said: 'His baby is in the hospital.' And I kind of looked at him, as if I hadn't understood, though I had, and I could see he was about to repeat himself and so I said: 'Why? What happened?' and he said: 'Apparently it had a series of seizures.' 'Jesus.' 'And now it's in a coma . . .' And I sort of reeled, looked up at the sky and took a step back—though to be honest it wasn't, like, a genuine reaction but rather my attempt to appear genuinely taken aback, which is not to say I wasn't truly shocked or terrified to hear this, but rather that it didn't genuinely elicit the reaction I, like, conjured for it. And I said: 'Do they know what's wrong?'

And my counselor said: 'No. Not yet. It may have hit its head. But your father and I decided to let you know now, that this is ongoing and that he'll call with any updates . . .' and then he cleared his throat and added: 'Though, of course, as is always the case, it's up to you if you feel you need to leave and be with your family . . . though I—and your father—seriously encourage you to stay.' And I hate to admit that I felt this, like, opening, and I started to say: 'Well, I mean . . .' But my counselor interrupted me to say: 'There's not really anything you can do for them, to be honest, other than continue to take care of yourself. And in fact, the best way to help them, to help your father, might be to stay here, where he knows you're safe, so as not to add to his anxiety.' And this made a great deal of sense to me, like perfect, rational sense, but I scrunched up my face as if to illustrate that maybe it didn't. And then before I could say anything my counselor reached out and touched my shoulder and said: 'Look, it's already late in the day, so why don't you take tonight to think about it and make a decision tomorrow. But please, think about it, and think about what I said.' And I nodded and touched his forearm in a gesture that I hoped connoted gravity and my awareness of the grave factors at play. And then we parted ways and on the way back to my unit I saw some of the guys throwing a frisbee on the lawn and I sat in the sun and watching them and ended up getting sunburned and being in a pretty great deal of discomfort.

"And that night I started to pack my things, because the truth was I needed to be there for my dad and my stepmom and to make sure I got to see the baby in case something happened . . . but also I just wanted to leave CVCAT and now I had a really good excuse. I didn't have a lot of stuff since my mom had packed for me while I was in the psych ward and must have done so somewhat distractedly since I ended up with only three pairs of underwear and three pairs of socks and a pair of pants and a coat and then, like, twelve t-shirts. And so I threw all these things into my bag and set the bag on Terry's empty bed and then stood there holding *The Long Pig*, kind of debating if I should take it with me since I was only like a quarter way through then and honestly wasn't sure I would ever finish it but also liked the idea of having it around for some reason. Like I kind of imagined myself sitting and reading it at a sidewalk table outside a bar, nursing a beer . . . though that was preposterous, because I couldn't drink anymore, and so I imagined myself reading it on a bench in the park, maybe taking occasional pulls from a one-hitter, which was different since I'd never really had a problem with weed the way I had a problem with alcohol and other things. Though to be honest I wasn't convinced that the problem was actually with alcohol and stuff as opposed to, like, just a nasty bout of depression brought on by having not resolved or grappled with the Bad Stuff, and I really thought that someday, once I'd found a little stability in my life, a little closure, I'd be able to drink once in a while, maybe even do a couple lines every now and then with friends. Because the truth was is I was not an addict—at least not the way these other guys were—but just that I'd gone through a rough patch and used drugs and alcohol as a crutch, which, obviously, didn't help, but which, like, once I no longer had the injury, and no longer needed the crutch, I would be able to use those things more healthily and normally. That was the thinking then, anyway.

"So I ended up putting *The Long Pig* in my bag under my clothes and undressed and got in bed—and I kept having to flip the pillow because it got warm under my head and the heat irritated my sunburn—and I laid there for awhile rehearsing how I was going to announce to my counselor that I had made up my mind to go home. And I kept landing on this one phrase: 'God forbid the baby doesn't get better . . .' which felt like sort of the best and most reasonable argument I had for leaving and one that my counselor really couldn't rightfully argue with. And so I built the rest of the speech or explanation or whatever around that phrase, ending up with what felt like a pretty solid thing, and I felt confident that by the next afternoon I would be out of this place, and replanted in my life as if nothing had ever happened.

"And as I lay there I started to have this really bizarre thought, like almost this kind of fantasy, about there being this person—and I couldn't decide if they were a man or a woman or whatever—kind of crouched in the corner of the room, at the foot of Terry's bed, wearing this big ratty black sweater that was pulled over their knees and their arms were inside the sweater so that the sweater's arms dangled there like hoses or something. And they were just staring at me with this sort of focused, frustrated look and I could see that their hands were, like, rummaging around inside the sweater, digging for something, and then all of a sudden they froze—still just looking at me, their eyes these dilated pits as black as their hair—and then their fingers peeped out from the sweater's neck hole and there was something in the fingers, a little beige clump of something, and they proceeded to delicately insert the clump into their mouth and chew it really gingerly and then swallow as if they were swallowing a huge pill or something and their face sort of contorted into this grimace, and then the fingers disappeared again into the sweater and the rummaging continued and they just kept staring at me from across the room. And I lay there and had this whole vision play out and knew I could stop it from happening, like just shift my thoughts to something else, but for some reason I let it keep going, almost as if I really *couldn't* stop it, though of course I could, but yet I just let it go on as if I couldn't. And it went on and on and on until the door clicked open, which triggered the whole thing to suddenly dissolve.

"And RN Simone was standing in the doorway. For the first time her hair was unbound, a like feral halation of black that flooded the doorway and assembled on top of her shoulders like dark water. Her turquoise scrubs seemed a size too small, or as if she had expanded inside them, and her hands wrung the bottom of her shirt. And she looked from me to the suitcase on Terry's bed, then back at me and said: 'Are you going somewhere?' And I sat up halfway and said: 'I'm leaving tomorrow.' And she stepped into the room and the door drifted shut behind her and as it did I felt my chest tighten. And she said: 'Already?' And I said: 'I have a family emergency.' And RN Simone sort of stopped mid-step, and her hands kneaded the front of her shirt, and she said: 'Oh no.' And I said: 'How are *you*?' And she took another step, so that she was only three or so paces from the bed—and I became distinctly conscious that I was in only my underwear—and she said: 'I'm alright. Better than yesterday.' And I said: 'What happened, anyway, that stressed you out?' And she sighed and tilted her head so that her hair drooped off her shoulder, and she stood with her hips cocked and her thick waist angled up to her right, as if trying to indicate something in the corner of the room. And she said: 'It really isn't appropriate for me to talk about other clients, but since you're leaving . . . When I was doing room checks last night I walked in on one of the guys . . . you know . . .' And I shifted my weight and said: 'I see . . .' and she said: 'And it wasn't, like, an accident, you know? He knew I was coming and he didn't, like, stop when I came in . . .' And I said: 'That's awful I'm so sorry.' And she said: 'It's alright. I think I overreacted. I mean, I've seen worse.' And I turned a palm upward and shrugged, to indicate that I believed her. And she continued: 'It was also just that it was, like, *that* particular guy,' she stuck out her tongue and feigned a gag. 'Like it's not something I wanted to see *him* doing . . .' she twisted at her shirt and for a moment I saw a sliver of flesh. 'I imagine not,' I said. She cocked her hips in the other direction, and her sneakers creaked, and she said: 'I mean it wouldn't have been so bad if it was someone else . . .' And I said: 'Right.' And she said: 'Like . . . if it had been, say, like, *you* . . . I mean . . .' and here her eyes sort of flittered across me and she said: 'I mean, that wouldn't have been too bad . . . Or bad at all . . .' And I adjusted my weight on the bed and said: 'Oh yeah?' And she took another step—two steps—until she was merely an inch or two from the bed, and she said: 'I wish we'd met under different circumstances.' And all I could do was nod sort of gravely, because I agreed so sincerely, and even more than that I felt this, like, rush of validation, this sense that I had been right all along—about everything. And RN Simone sort of swayed her hips and twisted her shirt and her lips gathered around her teeth and her hair was a mass of shadows and she lifted a leg and propped her knee on the edge of my mattress so the cool, ductile material of her scrubs brushed my bare thigh, and she said: 'I guess, since this is your last night, we could pretend that you're not, you know, what you are . . .' And I said: 'Yeah, I'm not.' And she said: 'Can you erase that horrible image I have from last night?' And I nodded and she stood there kind of poised over my bed and watched me, and she wrested her shirt and rocked on her knee and I watched her watching me and felt this sense of being somehow magnified in her eyes, and I focused on not finishing, because I knew that when I did the sensation would vanish, but it was more and more difficult not to because the way she was watching me—and her knee against my thigh and now her hand in my hair—was just insanely exciting and I reached the point where I had to let go, to take my hand off it because otherwise it would have been over. And when I did she took the hand—took both the hands—and guided them to her, put them on her scrubs, and they seized the scrubs, kneaded and wrung and wrested the scrubs up and down and aside and her smell came out and she smelled like sweat and smoke and disinfectant—and later—I don't know how much later exactly because time was widening and narrowing like water through the pipes of a building, and the sheets were torn from the rangy mattress, and I held her arms out straight behind her, locked in place, and her hands were knotted together as if they were one hand and her face entangled in the lake of her black hair, and every time I thrust the flesh on her back rippled away from me, or toward me—I glanced at one point toward the door, which was ajar, and rows of taut eyes bared inward, and there was whispering, rapid and urgent and consonant, and I looked back at the eyes, unblinking, and I smiled so widely that my sight tapered, and I came.

"And when I fell asleep I dreamed about standing in the sunlight watching a dark shape lumber through the sky, like a hole cut into the blue, guttering, demonstrable . . . And when I woke up—and RN Simone was still there, her turquoise scrubs in a knot on the floor, her hair spattered across the bed and cut with bars of light from through the blinds—I wondered if the dream was, like, I don't know, somehow, like . . . But it doesn't matter, because all that's . . . you know."

X Parke's toes curl and she traces a line along Malory's thigh's warm skin. "Why are you trying to make me jealous?"

"I'm not. I'm sorry."

"Well you did." The blankets move. "You said you have . . . Bad Stuff."

"Yeah."

"I think I might too. Maybe."

"Yeah."

"Maybe."

"At least we get to have Bad Stuff together," Malory's hands flitter briefly.

"You like having Bad Stuff with me?"

"I like having Bad Stuff with you."

"I like having Bad Stuff with you too."

6

X Parke's having this dream in which she's climbing down this spiraling stairwell and the stairwell's steps and walls and ceiling are mantled in this lush velvety fabric the color of the inside of a mouth and all very soft and silent, X Parke stepping down step by step and barefoot so she feels the soft warmth of the velvety red fabric on her soles and glides her fingers along the stairwell's equally soft warm wall as she goes. Silence. She doesn't know how far down the stairwell helicoids nor what's at its bottom, but she's just grateful that she's walking down and not up. She thinks she remembers the stairwell's mouth, somewhere overhead, which she thinks sprung from a narrow room with dark glass and gaudy blandishments and a low leather-upholstered bench along one wall and a long fish tank built into the wall over the bench with a single eyeless fish sculling stilly nowhere—but she may be remembering something else from some other dream. There's this distinct familiarity too to the stairwell's helix, and to the red velvet overlay, and even and especially to the descent. X Parke's not convinced that she's asleep but also knows this isn't her real life; the concentrated silence convinces her thus; the whole thing's too quiet to be real life. And if it *is* real life then it's not behaving the way it's supposed to. Real life is supposed to have sound, even the largely imperceptible but ubiquitous wafting of the air's molecules whereas here in this well of lush red velvet there's no wafting, as if the air here's molecules have gone static or entropied or otherwise disappeared. Silent and sealed like a world on the page. Though none of this interrupts or dissuades X Parke from continuing downward step by soft step on her bare feet with a hand on the soft red wall and a decoction of red glowing below where the stairwell spirals into a curdling redness which though X Parke doesn't know what's down there she's left thinking about, the bottom of the stairwell, even after waking up in the matted AM light with the blankets and Malory's limbs braided through her and the fire out, blinking up at the gray-blue ceiling which has absolutely no red in it at all.

Malory issues a consonant word or words and wakes up sweating and tremulous. He whispers about the dream he had, in which he says he was looking out the window of his father's apartment at the park and the buildings beyond as fire rained from a clear sky and flooded the park and the city with flames. He was so scared, he says, that he was going to die. There were other people with him and all they could do was watch through the window as the fire rained down and he says the worst part was that it was daytime and the sky was clear and he could see the park and the buildings and everything burning so plainly, just burning in the sunlight. He sort of pauses and squishes his eyes shut and traces the spiral on his neck with the knuckle of a thumb and suspires then says, "And we were talking about what could be happening, like what could cause this, and someone said it was an accident like some kind of factory or industrial accident or something and I or someone else said back, 'What kind of industrial accident could make the world end?' and the first person responded that it wasn't one of *our* factories, it wasn't *our* industrial accident, and I said, '*What?*' and they said, 'Not *ours*. Not *our* accident.' And at that point the fire was raining down in sheets and the flames were almost at the window which is five stories up and so I started looking around for some way to kill myself before I burned alive and everyone started trying to stop me, as if there was a way we were gonna make it out of this, and I tried to get away from them to go have privacy and kill myself but they held me down and piled on top of me and I couldn't see or breathe and all I heard were their voices which were chanting something in unison and then I was or now I am here." He swallows and grimaces and drinks the remaining water, and X Parke has to go outside—the sky's trellised in high webby clouds and very cold—and pack snow into the plastic gallon and then set the gallon near the fireplace and then jimmy a couple legs from a chair and get the fire going again all while Malory's under the blankets occasionally whimpering. X Parke strokes the section of blankets beneath which she assumes is a shoulder and asks him what he needs. "Booze," his voice wrestles from underneath about an octave up from where it's usually, X Parke patting the shoulder and saying, “I know,” and then heading off to find somewhere to pee that isn’t the frigid outdoors and settling on the immediate cusp of a hallway off the foyer and going right on the deco carpet, and while squatting gazing off from the hallway’s cusp back through the foyer at another hallway opposite and seeing there just at the far hallway’s mouth what appears to be a prism on the floor seething weak light. She goes to it, peeking into Malory’s room where he’s still dissembled in blankets, past the long mealy western-facing curtains, and finds that the prism, as she pauses at the hallway’s cusp, is actually an empty bottle quavering delicately on the carpet, and next to it is another one, and another next to that, and more beyond until X Parke’s eyes adjust and the entire hallway’s length’s infested with empty bottles as far as she can see until darkness crashes over. Each bottle is replete with a strip of masking tape across which ‘WHISKEY’ is printed as if with a sharpie. X Parke’s chewing a fingernail and trying to count the bottles and considering also Malory’s account of his duration here in this abandoned hotel—“a week or so”—and trying to ally that duration with this amount of bottles and finding a major discrepancy there, whereas she can see and count three dozen+ bottles before they recede into shadow and so that’s thirty-six bottles across say even generously fourteen days, meaning—X Parke’s fingers flap—that’s two and a half bottles a day, these bottles being the large fifths she thinks they’re called, a likely fatal quantity of alcohol, and again that’s only what she can see here, now bending and picking up the nearest bottle and tossing it down the hall into the shadows from where a moment later there's a chorus of clanks and clangors and X Parke wipes her palms on the front of her hoodie. The reasonable explanation is very reasonable, it being that these bottles do not belong to Malory or certainly not all of them. This hotel's been abandoned for probably years and years, and so of course other people've passed through and stayed awhile, maybe likely too a group of people, a group of heavy drinkers roaming together through the forest and discovering this hotel and inhabiting it together for months to erect this very frankly morbid altar to consumption. There's no other explanation. One dude couldn't drink all this, certainly not in a week or so. And how even would he've gotten all these bottles in here to begin with? X Parke nods here in the hallway's cusp, nods toward the hallway's shadow, from which of course is silence which should sustain indefinitely given that it's only her and Malory here in the ruins of this sprawling hotel and Malory's all wound into his blankets in the other room. But instead what happens now is there's a clatter from the hallway's far shadow, and another nearer, and from the shadow the bottles birl and ripple with decreasing impetus toward X Parke until only a tinny shiver purrs near her feet and dies. She doesn't breathe or anything. The clatter comes again, and X Parke backsteps from the hallway into the foyer and pauses, squints toward the dark where the bottles bristle, and there just inside the shadow's threshold something wades forward on two legs with turquoise skin and arms cocked at these flamboyant almost operatic angles, then stops there completely still, holding this extravagant pose, mostly still obscured in the shadow and but there are the whites of teeth and eyes and a thuck of shadow around the head and X Parke swallows and I sidle her carefully backward and return her to the other room where she crouches beside the knot of blankets and touches them and says, "Is there someone else here?"

A burp or a cough comes from inside the blankets and Malory's voice: ". . . will you help me die . . ."

The little hairs on X Parke's body stiffen. "What?"

The blankets depress.

"I won't," X Parke smoothing the blankets, watching the doorless doorway where beyond the foyer's light is gray and everything is OK. "Is that really what you want?"

Something dislodges and clatters inside the wall behind the fireplace, clatters past the floor and below, X Parke thinking now about whatever dusty chambers cower underfoot, low ceilings furried with mold.

"Are all those bottles yours?" she asks.

The blankets grunt in either bashful affirmative or adamant refusal. X Parke burrows into the blankets where it's humid and smells like breath and Malory's still undressed and his skin's cold and damp and taut across his dimpling bones, X Parke tucking the blankets shut behind her and balling against Malory's crooked body and falling promptly asleep, here now at the same time Malory burrowing out from the blankets and propping himself up on an arm and blinking very muscularly at where the girl's little body barely distinguishes itself from the blankets' innate folds. He yawns shakily, his ribs announcing themselves from the trap of his skin, then gathers a wad of clothes until he's carrying what he suspects constitutes a complete outfit and goes out into the foyer and dresses, finding he's only missing socks. He spits and lights and smokes his way to the hotel's entrance's tall oak doors and cracks them and wedges out onto the icy porch. The valley's shut in perfect snow and so quiet because there's no other people. Other people are repellent. Malory prefers himself. He stands rooted to the ice by his soles and waits with his body tucked inside his Carhartt and his heart beating kind of sideways, as if caught on something, and his head and throat and eyes are sore. Also he's having memory issues; he thinks he might've been talking half-asleep; and there was a dream that's gone now; he can't remember the girl's name, some initials. Last night he was glad to have her, though now he wants his privacy back. But maybe she'll leave on her own without him having to ask or demand—assuming she's even real. He flicks his cigarette in what he intends to be a graceful arc but which cambers sideways and pitters down the porch's steps. He's gonna need more booze and soon, is what he's thinking mostly: more booze and soon or else. But what's he gonna do? The cellar's cleaned out. Cleaned the fuck out. It was an unmitigated miracle to find that place, stocked like that, more than he could drink in a lifetime, he thought. And alas. Here he is: Same lifetime, no more to drink. How'd this happen? And now he's in a lot of trouble. He can feel his breath's wrong, and his hands are light. And of course all the other stuff, the mental stuff. He needs to find more. Maybe there's more in another larder in the cellar, an untapped larder with as much or more whiskey than the first one, even vodka or fucking wine he'll take whatever. It's worth a try. He stopped looking after all, after finding the whiskey. Maybe there's another larder. There's probably another larder. It's worth a try. There's definitely another larder, and if there's not it doesn't matter anyway because nothing matters, anyway.

The girl's still asleep and he tries to be quiet but the hotel's floorboards creak even if you just look at them wrong, and Malory keeps pausing as he makes his way across the foyer and manages to get all the way to the far southeast hallway without waking her as far as he can tell. When he'd first found this hotel Malory'd been loath to explore much, still having back then the few handles he'd gotten in town and which he expected to last him until he moved on. But they hadn't of course and within days he was dry and simultaneously the weather got vicious and stayed vicious and really maybe for no other reason than to distract himself from the shaking and the anxiety he'd started poking around, finding at first nothing but tottering rooms with occasional rotting furniture and dark ramous hallways that never ended and to the northwest an entire wing or ell charred and black and thatched with fallen joists and ossified doors. But then he'd discovered the cellar, accessed via the hallway now strewn with the empties he now attempts to avoid stepping on but which gradually become so dense and in the hallway's darkeningness he ends up kicking a few into a few others and they clank angrily, but then soon there are no more bottles and Malory feels his way along the hallway's wall with an arm outstretched until the wall bends sharply and bends sharply again, and here he toes in the dark for the edge of the soft top step of the stairwell that will lead him to the cellar. There is an odor that he hadn't noticed last time he'd been down this way, of copper maybe, which is unpleasant enough that he pauses to light a cigarette and scowls into the dwindling pack and then advances step-by-step downward with a hand on the soft wall to his right and the other hand outspread in front of him in case anything should be dangling from the ceiling like cobwebs or something else that he doesn't want in his mouth or hair or eyes. The stairs buckle steeply back and forth, Malory having a poor sense of the stairwell's depth without his sight and counting steps for the first thirty then getting bored and just going on. Back when he was a kid, when his parents were still together and before all the Bad Stuff, his family'd had a dog, a red German Spaniel with a docked tail, who was a year older than Malory—his parents swore—to the day. This dog, whose name Malory cannot remember, had vibrant heterochromatic eyes, one atmosphere-blue and the other jack-o-lantern orange, and a distinct birthmark on its tongue in the shape of what always struck Malory as an island, Malory as a child often imagining the tongue as a treasure map and the island-birthmark the location of some magnificent treasure, the nature of which, given young Malory's predilection for manga and video games, tended to be some kind of divine and dreadful weapon with which he would someday rule the world if only he could figure out which island on an atlas resembled the one on the dog's tongue. When the dog died—Malory was twelve or thirteen—his family had it cremated and drove out of the city to a nature preserve upstate and dumped the ashes in a little heap so much smaller than the dog had been, and Malory remembers wondering if that heap of brown ashes could possibly be the whole dog, whose name, again, he cannot remember now as the stairwell steepens and he's forced to use his lighter, tensing with the cost of each second's burned fluid in exchange for just a meager pocket of orange light sculpted from the otherwise interminable dark, holding the lighter toward the stairwell's soft red walls and then down and forward where the soft red steps spiral down. Malory remembers returning to the apartment after leaving the dog's ashes upstate, and his parents sitting him down and explaining to him that they were no longer in love and were going to separate for a while or probably forever, Malory remembering his dad grinning in this way that made him think the whole thing was a joke, the announced separation and maybe even the dog's death and the whole world, since in fact his dad loved to play jokes or pranks on him when he was young. But this particular joke never ended, not the separation nor the dead dog nor the world. Malory walks downward on his bare feet with the lighter suspended sort of nebulously ahead where its pocket of light just barely grazes the visceral red walls to either side of him and just hardly skirts the visceral red steps that gyre down much further than he remembers at a dizzying acuity. There was something else about the dog that he wants to remember but can't quite get to, something about its character that was important, or is important, but just isn't coming to him. It was a good dog, whatever its name was. Malory misses it, right now, a little.

He remembers this one joke or prank his dad played on him and with which his mom abetted when he was maybe seven years old where after school he'd come home and his mom and dad were there and very excited about something and brought him into the living room and told him that he was going to have a new baby brother or sister which is something Malory'd thought couldn't happen for some reason and about which he wasn't sure how he felt there as his parents sat across from him beaming in a way that signaled to Malory something about how they felt about him, as in why would they be beaming thus at the prospect of a new child if the current child was all the things he was supposed to be, and but maybe this was just how people were supposed to act in this situation and so he'd done his best to mirror their beams and they'd told him too that he couldn't tell anyone, not even the other kids at school or especially any teachers and Malory promised not to tell and then life went on with just the three of them and Malory's mom's belly started to get bigger and she left the apartment less often and fewer people came by to visit until it was pretty much just her there all the time and Malory's dad going to work and coming right home and Malory going to school and coming right home and one day Malory'd come home from school and heard his mom in the bedroom and so'd gone in to ask her to make him food and when he'd walked in she was there having just gotten out of the shower because her black hair was dripping and so naturally wasn't wearing any clothes and her belly, which by then was pretty huge when she waddled around the apartment, was flat there with no clothes on, and she'd turned her back to Malory and told him to wait in the kitchen and he'd gone and sat in the kitchen and soon his mom'd came in and she was dressed now in sweatpants and a sweater and her belly was again huge and bulbous and she'd made him food and asked him about his day as if nothing out of the ordinary had transpired to such a degree that Malory started to suspect he'd mis-seen or else that pregnancy just worked that way where the belly was only big when the pregnant person was wearing clothes and was flat otherwise. Anyway and so now here the steps steepen further and narrow further so Malory's only able to get half a bare foot on each step and he holds the lighter down to see where he's going as best he can, and when finally his mom was ready to give birth to this brother or sister she'd gone into the bedroom with Malory's dad and closed the door and Malory'd stood in the hallway listening to the shrieks and swears of his mom and his dad intoning monosyllables and this went on for maybe an hour or two with the shrieks getting more and more blood-curdling and the swears growing more and more obscene and the dad's intoning becoming more and more deadpan until finally it all stopped and there was silence and Malory had his little seven year old hands knotted into the waistband of his pants and then the bedroom door opened and his mom and dad walked slowly out and his dad was holding a wad of clothes and he kneeled in front of Malory and held out the wad and told Malory to take a look and so he'd reached out very tentatively because he didn't want to hurt the baby brother or sister with his bigger hands and he'd peeled back the clothes here and there and spread them open and looked down into them and there was nothing except more clothes and he'd not understood what was happening and so looked up at his dad who was grinning in the way he always did when he'd just played a prank or joke and his mom was grinning too only not as triumphantly and maybe a little somber or sullen and his dad'd said "Gotchya" and laughed and his mom'd chuckled and Malory did his best to mirror their amusement. Now here the staircase narrowing further so that Malory has to turn sideways and kind of grapevine down the steps and the cigarette's still in his mouth but a hot nub now and he's not sure what to do with it because the soft stairwell's possibly flammable and his feet are bare and so he just keeps it in his mouth as he squeezes down with his lighter outheld in the direction he's going and the stairwell's so narrow it's pressing on his front and back until he feels all of a sudden the space ahead open up and the temperature drop and he steps off the soft last step onto smooth cold floor and there's faint red light ahead and toward which, after crushing the nubby cigarette on the hard floor, he goes now without his lighter's light and he can feel as he shakes the lighter before putting it in his pocket it's been reduced nearly to fumes.

Soon the red light widens and Malory's back in the circular room with the pitted stone walls and the stone pillar at the center with the fire still burning inside the mouth at its base and the five doorways to the five larders sited around the room's perimeter. The whiskey'd been on shelves in the damp larder behind the first door to his right, the first and last door he'd opened. There was no reason to continue looking after that; there was nothing else he could imagine wanting to find. Now he checks that larder behind that first door again, just in case one or two bottles remain tucked in the corners or below the dusty shelves or hiding behind the doorframe. But it's empty. He cleaned it, as he already knows, the fuck out. That leaves four more doors, the second from the right which Malory's now approaching, fingering the outline of his cigarette pack through the front of his jeans and shaking his head in rehearsal for the inevitable disappointment, pulling back the door which creaks and shaking his head as he squints inside at a glistening wall of bottles, registering not immediately what he's seeing but instead recalling a joke he'd heard about an alcoholic who's walking along a beach and finds a magic lamp from which pops a genie who grants him three wishes, the alcoholic thinking for less than an instant before saying "I wish I had a bottle of booze that never runs dry," and so abracadabra and poof he's holding a bottle full of whiskey which he guzzles until his stomach's veritably bursting and then looks at the bottle and finds it still completely full. And the genie goes "And what are your other two wishes?" and the alcoholic again without hesitation says "I'll take two more of these." Malory's shaking head now graduating into a nodding one as the second door's contents start to sort of swim into fruition, there being here as already noted a wall of bottles, these like the bottles in the first larder when he'd found them full of whiskey and labeled each with a little strip of masking tape with the word 'WHISKEY' hand-printed there, except in this larder there appear to be like ten times as many bottles from the first larder whereas in the first larder the larder's shelves were lined pretty densely with bottles constituting a total of maybe forty of fifty bottles but whereas in this new larder the bottles are crammed into every space herein, stacked atop one another in a way that Malory's too in awe to realize is not physically feasible given the bottles' wide bases and narrow necks, and whereas there were forty or fifty bottles of whiskey in the previous larder there may well be four or five hundred herein, Malory now reaching up to a near one and taking it down and smiling without realizing he's smiling at just the weight of it in his hand and popping out the loosely wedged cork and smelling, almost starting to cry here in the circular cellar and taking a long drink. His heart levels out and his hands kind of ground themselves and his mood just improves all at once and to such a degree that he forgets instantly how sick and sad he'd felt a second before. Maybe he can get the girl to help him carry all this upstairs, she'll probably do whatever he asks. He drinks and peers into the larder via the hole left by the bottle he's removed, and there are rows of additional bottle receding into shadow and also, lined on the shelves, unless he's mistaken . . . and here he pulls a few more bottle and sets them on the stone floor, one cracking and spilling there but about which Malory merely shrugs since there's so much more, in order to make room for an arm which he now snakes through the opening and feels along the shelves and feels what he thinks he saw and draws it out, and looks here down at it and shakes his head again this time incredulously, peels open the carton's side and fingers out a pack—his brand—drops the carton to the floor and jams an arm back into the larder and fishes out another carton, and another, now taking a long gulp, two, from a bottle and lighting a cigarette and smoking and drinking and lining the bottles along the floor and stacking the cartons of cigarettes beside them and not even bothering to count because there's enough of everything that he'll never run out of anything ever again.

Finally pausing and turning toward the third door, his vision sort of fisheying on account of the whiskey and feeling warm and so happy, now going to the third door figuring that he should account for all the bottles and cigarettes down here at once and just clean the place out and get it all upstairs so he'll never have to come down here again and can just sit by the fireplace and drink and smoke all winter and probably through the spring and summer and into the fall, and with the mostly empty bottle dangling in his hand and a cigarette in the other he opens the third door, already nodding preemptively at his incredible fortune, and but now frowns and scoffs as behind the third door there's only darkness and nothing and he looks back at the rows and lines of bottles and cartons from the previous larder to verify they're still there, and then looks back into the third larder and blinks and cranes forward and sees there in the shadowy back of the larder something just barely perceptible, a shape stirring there and coming forward and the sound of bells or wind chimes and Malory backsteps and drops the bottle which clanks on the stone floor and rolls semicircularly drooling an arc of whiskey, Malory's back now flush against the cellar's central pillar and the shape still approaching from the larder, now coming into the faint light and there's turquoise and a surge of black around the face and Malory's pulse gambols and his eyebrows curve. "What are you doing here?" he breathes, dragging on his cigarette instinctually and matting his hair back from his face.

"Are you making up stories about me, thirsty boy?" the portion of RN Simone's mouth that Malory can see below the hair moving in discordance with the voice and the voice different than Malory remembers though it's possible he's misremembering the voice and the crepitating one he hears now is the right voice because his memory's all messed up anyway and he doesn't trust anything he thinks he knows.

"I'm not I'm not," he's saying, one hand flush against a cheek and grinning in a way that makes him look, he would think could he see himself, like his dad.

RN Simone stops in the doorway and jerks her hips sidewise and raises her arms up over her head as if just pre-bow-post-opera and rasping, "So we did all the things," through the thicket of black hair, now sort of shambling forward in such a way that her feet seem not to carry her weight appropriately, her limbs and hair swaying and Malory actually scrunching up his eyes and laughing because he doesn't know what to say or do and laughter feels as warranted as anything else, RN Simone also close enough now that Malory can smell her and she smells just like he imagined like smoke and sweat and disinfectant and also something else, something different underneath that Malory cannot place but does not like and all this tension and desire rushing through him and making him feel almost homesick though why would he be homesick for a rehab and anyway now with most of her face still obscured by hair RN Simone says "Did we do all the things, thirsty boy?" and Malory swallowing and shrugging and pressed up against the pillar which is warm from the fire in its base and RN Simone approaching further in this tussled manner so she's only a foot or so away from him and she says "Do you want to do all the things to me?" and Malory laughs again with his cigarette so nubby it singes the outside of his fingers and falls out of his hand all without him registering and he can do nothing except nod rapidly and place his palms flat on the pillar's warm stone, RN Simone saying "You can have everything you want, thirsty boy," and dropping abruptly to her knees before him so her head lolls and her fingers bunch on the ground, "What do you want from me? You can have it," and Malory here with his vision skewed and his belly hot and blood pooling in his crotch kind of clears his throat and starts to speak but his throat is still muddied and so clears it again and says "I want you to watch me," and feels his face redden and but without any hesitation now one of RN Simone's hands is pawing clumsily at the front of his jeans and the tennis ball-green fingernails are struggling to locate the buttons and zippers and Malory brushes them away and undoes his pants and holds it there as RN Simone collapses back onto her haunches and her head tilts and she's completely still and Malory watches her as she watches him through her hair and he's breathing heavily and his foot slides and strikes the empty bottle and sends it rolling off across the floor and he feels himself tautening in his hand while his other hand flexes against the warm stone pillar and now all at once RN Simone ragdolls forward and slams her face against Malory's penis and the penis gouges and bounces around the cool damp face until it finds a hole and the hole engulfs the penis and Malory grasps RN Simone's black hair in both fists and feeds the penis into the hole and at one point rocks his head back in ecstasy and collides it with the pillar which sends wiry hot tendrils through his brain and blunts his sight but he merely smiles and feels himself pulsing and RN Simone says "Anything you want, thirsty boy," as if her mouth is unobstructed and so he casts her backward and falls on top of her and rips her scrubs aside so her breasts flop out and he kneads them and kneads her belly and yanks down the pants and a raw smell comes out that reminds him of something, of the Bad Stuff, but he cannot stop now and he enters her and thrusts with his face scrunched shut and whiskey fumes gathering behind his face and RN Simone intones "Yes, thirsty boy. Yes," and Malory's teeth are gritting and his fingers clawing at the shoulders and hair and he feels himself start to cum and so pulls out and tries to flip RN Simone over but she feels caught on something, Malory pulling her harder so her hair jerks aside and he sees the face which is not the face he remembers RN Simone having but just some face, some face with a hole where its left side should be, and Malory gasps and sees there protruding from her back a braid of wires extending into the dark end of the larder where now, blinking, Malory can see something crouching and the glint of an animal's eyes swathed in earthy fur, and Malory scrambles sideways and collides with the next door and RN Simone or the thing he thought was RN Simone is violently yanked and dragged back into the larder and there's a chittering laugh and the clatter of bells and Malory closes his eyes and shoots himself in the head while his penis stands there bleeding a bead of semen, and a minute elapses now with Malory slouched against the fourth door without realizing he's slouched against the fourth door until there's a terse rap on it from the inside, at which Malory leaps away and collapses against the pillar with his pants still down and the rap comes again and a voice "Mal? Mal? Are you okay?" and Malory sniffles and blinks and says "Mom?" and yet does not move and the voice comes again "Mal let me out. Let me help you," and Malory upturns his face and releases a single sob and then crawls to the fourth door and twists the knob and lets it open and his mom rushes through in her sweatpants and sweatshirt with her round belly and crouches beside him, cradling his head and saying "Why are you telling people bad stuff happened to you?" and Malory's dad comes through the doorway now and stands over them looking piteously down with his lips tucked into his teeth and tears leak out of Malory's eyes and he says "I'm so sorry," and his mom says "Nothing bad ever happened don't lie," and pulls a wad of tissues from the neck of her sweater and her black hair cascades down onto Malory's face and she says "Let's clean the lying baby" and uses the tissues to dab at Malory's still tumescent penis while his dad now squats beside him and takes his hand and Malory cries and groans and says "Thank you thank you" and holds his dad's hand while his mom dabs and rubs at his penis with increasing rigor, screaming a burst of gibberish at him and pursing her lips and narrowing her eyes through the curtains of her hair and saying "You've made such a tangled mess," and rubbing harder now with both hands and Malory cries and looks away and lurches as he ejaculates a gasp of smoke and fire and feels his dad's hand tighten around his and hears his mom's voice saying "There there," and there's a sudden rending shriek and Malory looks up where his mother's now holding a wad of clothes and wiggling her fingers like white worms over the wad and looking at the wad and not at Malory who looks at his dad's hand, which is steeped in layers of faded ink, and then up at his dad's face with its deep lines and the wide spaces between the teeth and the white ponytail dangling and his dad says, "You're doing really well," and Malory nods and tries to clear his stuffed nose by inhaling and exhaling briskly and his dad pats his chest and says "Let's get moving now," and Malory props himself up and buckles his pants and rises shakily and starts to reach for another bottle of whiskey but his dad holds up a tattooed hand and says "There's no time for that," and Malory sobs again and shuffles up to his dad who places a hand on his shoulder and says "We're going to tell everyone the truth," and gestures toward the fifth door, Malory breathing through his mouth, smelling his own fetid breath, regarding the fifth door through half-shut eyes while from the corner of his sight there's a brindled face peeking from the third door's frame and wideset eyes and his mom's sitting on the stone ground jerking the wad the clothes back and forth and his dad's hand's tracing tight circles on his back and nudging him forward, Malory now touching the fifth door's knob and thinking for some reason about a pall of birds startled from a tree by a sound except there is no sound in this imagining, just birds exploding from the boughs of a dead tree and blotting the sky, and he opens the fifth door and smells earthiness and feels the hot dry air and looks on through the door where there's a passage of fine dirt hewn by brittle hedges extending and branching into forks and overhead a sky thrashing flames and raining smoke, and Malory's dad prods Malory forward and says "Go tell them the truth," and Malory steps dejectedly through the doorway into the passage and his dad closes the door behind him and now turns and looks directly at me with the bare whites of his eyes though I have not shown myself or devised this and he winks and mouths a word whose white letters balloon from his mouth and harden in the air while the fire in the hole at the pillar's base crackles endlessly up the flue which buckles into a series of interlocking chimneys caked in soot and intermittent bat carcasses and leads eventually to the fireplace in the room off the foyer where X Parke's still tucked stilly beneath the blankets and now stirs and stretches them from her and blinks around, finding herself alone and the day's light riper than she'd left it, anxious to keep moving and calling Malory's name thrice at thirty-second intervals to no avail and so gathering some things—the plastic gallon of water and some snacks—and walking the room's perimeter to check for any stray belongings before heading through the foyer with her head down and out onto the old hotel's porch where she disarranges a smattering of bare footprints with her Converse without noticing them.

PART III

The Meadow and the Misread

7

Heading north now through the valley, only fifty-or-so paces from the hotel's entrance and there's an angle of hedges to X Parke's right conspicuously snowless among the otherwise snow-locked landscape. Nearing it the ground rises for her enough that she can discern from her heightened vantage it's a hedge maze. Within it, tangled reticulations of hedge. She walks the length of a side, counting twenty paces, then the adjacent side, counting twenty more. At the third side's middle she discovers an entrance, a 5ft wide gap in the hedge fitted with a gate fashioned from interlocking branches, and peering through the slats in the gate she sees the maze's first passage, off which she counts three additional passages forking, and she nudges softly at the gate and is amused when it glides easily and soundlessly open. She stands just outside the maze and, by way of humoring herself and offsetting some placeless guilt she's feeling all of a sudden start to curdle in her belly, she calls, "Malory?" into the maze and drums her fingers along the gate.

There's a squawk overhead and X Parke cranes up to look but sees nothing but seething white sky and then a voice comes from the maze. "Hello?" it sounds as if from very distant. X Parke lets the gate close and stands at the gate frowning and holding the gallon of water in the crook of an arm. Through the gate nothing moves and the passage forks. Seconds elapse and X Parke touches the gate and then withdraws her hand and steps back, then calls, "Malory?" again.

"Is someone there?" the voice calls back. "Oh please let someone be there."

X Parke glances left and right at the maze's exterior's hedge and affixes her hair away from her face. "Yes," she says too quietly, and clears her throat, and registers now that the maze's interior, like its exterior hedges, is also snowless, the passages' floors bare dirt, and X Parke frowns further and chews her tongue around her mouth and tries to think of how and why this might be, the maze of course open on the top and everything else as far as X Parke can see—now triple checking and confirming—layered under deepish snow. She squats and reaches under the gate and touches the dirt just inside the maze, thinking maybe it's heated somehow, but it's as frigid as the snow just outside, which she notices now ends abruptly at the maze's boundary as if it's been shoveled or otherwise displaced rather than melted. And there's something else very strange about the maze, something X Parke rubs her eyes to verify, and blinks, and still can't believe. . . .

"Hello?" the voice calls from inside. "Someone?"

"Yes," X Parke says. "I'm here. I'm someone."

"Thank goodness. Thank goodness you're here."

"What are you doing in there, Malory?" X Parke outspreads a hand.

"I'm not Malory," says the voice, sounding now nearer than before.

X Parke steps back some paces from the maze's entrance. "Who are you, then?"

"My name's Harold. Harold Blyzniak. I've been lost in here for . . . for I don't know. Many *days*. I'm thirsty. I'm cold. Please, go fetch a staff person and ask them to get me out of here."

"A staff person?"

"One of the hotel's staff people. You know. The folks in the green collared shirts. They have little bronze nametags. They're everywhere. Please. I won't last another night in here. I'm so thirsty."

X Parke toes at the snow's boundary and looks back across the valley at the dilapidated hotel which besides being under snow she can tell is leaning and warped in sections, one ell downright mutilated so its cloak of snow is bulbous and spiky and there are no footprints anywhere other than X Parke's from the hotel's entrance to here, though as she's looking there are some occasional blemishes in the snow that may be footprints, perhaps one of a squirrel or even here along the far side of the maze some tracks that are vaguely deer-like, and intersecting her own footprints are the delicate scritches of a bird that must've scurried either one way or another after she passed, and there's an area over there where some of the snow looks like its been dug up and displaced in a neat little mound where something must have burrowed for food—but otherwise the snow is unmarred and certainly by *staff* footprints or human footprints of any kind, besides X Parke's.

"Hello? Someone?"

"Yes," X Parke touches the gate. "But . . . there's no staff here, I don't think. There's no *anyone* here, except me and my friend, Malory. But I don't know where Malory is and he definitely isn't staff." She swallows. "The hotel's kind of . . . abandoned."

There's a stretch of silence now during which X Parke considers it's likely she's being fucked with, probably by Malory but even by someone else, by this Harold Blyzniak, who's pranking her or otherwise messing with her with this *staff* stuff. And she considers that maybe she should be playing along by saying something like, "Oh, yes, a staff person. Why, the place is just teeming with staff people. Would you prefer a male or female? Or for that matter do you have a preference of age? There are just too many for me to choose. Should I ask them to fetch you a warm towel and have a meal delivered to your room? Or would you prefer some time in the spa after your *many days* lost in this maze?" But before she can say anything there's a low sob, which swells and widens into a howl, and which effectively conveys to X Parke she's misread the situation.

"I'm going to die in here," the voice howls. "I'm going to die in this maze and never be found. My wife will think I've abandoned her. My children will not remember me. I'll be spoken about with derision—if I'm spoken about at all. I never should have come in here. I had a bad feeling before I ever left my room. I should have gone to the pool. Or sat with a book by the fireplace."

X Parke's mind conjures or receives a spate of images: a flindering green door; a camp of bats dripping from rafters; the college's quad first empty, now speckled with students, now empty again and muddled with sunlight; four hands entwined, and the bulky silhouette of a barn backlit by the moon; X Parke's eyes trailing where a darting bird might go, tracing the maze's gate's ramiform shape and now settling on the gate's top, where a scuffed wooden board partially hidden behind a braid of hedge is engraved as if by hand with the phrase *Vide dans le vide.*

"But I should have known this maze was going to be a problem," says the voice of Harold Blyzniak. "There's something very troubling about it, I'm sure you've noticed."

"Yes . . ." X Parke chews a strip of lip skin.

"I know some about hedge mazes," he continues. "This particular maze is regarded architecturally as a three-dimensional, point-navigated, multicursal planair maze with both sparse and partial-braid routing. It contains zero bias, an 11.17/12° run factor, and was constructed using a multiple-solution, wall-adding technique. It has 17 dead ends. These particular components are relatively average in most hedge mazes. There exist, however, non-hedge mazes: two-dimensional mazes—as the ones done on paper with a pencil—as well as agent-type mazes that are *not* hedge mazes and adhere to differentiating components than this one. Though I can't think of an example right now."

"I'm confused," X Parke goes. "If you know so much about the maze, then how is it you're lost inside?"

"Because even Daedalus, who *built* his maze, became lost inside it. Though in his case I think the maze was actually a labyrinth, the distinction of which is often overlooked. See, labyrinths are unicursal, meaning there is a single throughway of twists and turns that eventually inevitably leads to an exit. They are expedients, artificial puzzles; walk far enough in a labyrinth and you will achieve a solution. Mazes on the other hand, like this one, are multicursal. They require choice and chance. Many routes herein are dead ends, and most lead away from an exit. Mazes are true puzzles, whereas labyrinths are illusions. Which I guess does not reflect well on Daedalus. Though in literature the terms tend toward interchangeability. It's possible Daedalus built a maze, which was referred to as a labyrinth for the sake of ostentation. See the words' lexicologies are mismatched and often misused. For example, the Tohon O'odham and Akimel O'odham, known anthropologically as the Pima, have stories of I'itoi, a mischievous god who resides in a cave beneath the Boboquivari Mountains. The tale is known colloquially as 'The Man in the Maze' but is frequently represented as an image of a figure standing at the mouth of a labyrinth. Further, the allegory is one pertaining to the *perceived* intricacies of life against the imminence of death and inevitable removal from the labyrinth. Though I for one appreciate—especially from in here—that life is riddled with true puzzles, choice and chance. There is something mazelike about every moment. And yet, of course, there is no real choice, since one will always inevitably reach the solution. Perhaps it's apt then to claim that while life is a labyrinth, living is a maze."

X Parke looks left up the valley, northward, where the valley extends unimpeded in more or less a straight line, and despite this she's instilled with the sensation you might have if someone's standing between you and something and you need the thing they're standing between you and, and she wonders how long she needs to stand here at the gates of this hedge maze and listen to Harold Blyzniak—whoever he is—before she can walk away without being rude.

"But I know enough about mazes that this shouldn't have happened," Harold's voice is continuing. "I know for example that a person inside a maze instructed to attempt an escape in as few turns as possible—but not necessarily in the shortest time possible—will tend to choose to take passages that appear to offer the greatest range of future choices, meaning more offshoots. Achitectural theorist Linda Binden proved this. She found that people correlate option with the potential for solution, mistakenly inferring that if a corridor offers more offshoots that it is more likely to produce a solution. Or that *those* offshoots will yield a greater degree of further offshoots and therefore potential solution etcetera. This implies a misled correlation between 'option' and 'solution.' Of course if the goal is to escape the maze, then necessarily all maze agents must incorrectly apply even this dubious logic at least *twice*, in order for the maze to be entered in the first place at all. As I did. And now I will likely die here, *en limnis*—'in the marsh'—or in 'the maze of tombs.' Mazes are frequently underground, grave-like chambers. Egyptians built maze complexes around the sarcophagi of their pharos to keep people out. Or to keep the pharos in. Like Skotino Cave and Gortyn. Procrustes of the Standard Bed. Jack Torrance in the Kubrick adaptation. Or the 'Chakravyuha,' supposed impregnable Indian battle formation described in the *Mahabhranta*. Churned through the belly of the beast. Intestinal, digesting me like food. *Hic inclusus, vitam perdit. Terra nullius . . .*"

"Why don't you just go through the hedges?" X Parke upturns a hand. "I mean, like, wrestle through them until you're out."

"The hedges are too sharp," Harold's voice is nearby. "I'll tear my skin off again."

X Parke grimaces. "I need to continue north," she says. "I'll send help, as soon as I can. If you can just hang on for a little longer . . ."

"I fear I have lost my humanness," Harold's voice is distant. "I fear I have lost the thing that endows humanness at all: imagination. Imagination of the divine. Noumenon. I fear I have forgotten how to *imagine* that there *exists* an outside of this maze at all. To imagine a non-maze space. How can I escape something that has no outside? I have become the Minotaur, with a head and therefore brain of a bull, incapable of the uniquely human imagining of a divine-outside. I am terrestrial. I know nothing but the buckling passages, regurgitating dimensions of this inside space.

There is nothing else. There *is* nothing else . . . That word, that silly little word, *is*. With all it's complications and compunctions, specifically the third-person singular present form as opposed to its more commonly discussed variants 'am,' 'are,' 'being,' 'been,' and of course, 'was' and 'were.' It is—hah—it is a grave irony, I realize now, to have devoted my life to the study of language, a pursuit I realize now was undertaken for reasons of strengthening my navigation of the maze of consciousness. Did I tell you I wrote my doctoral dissertation on collocation and semantic prosody?"

"What? No."

"I examined the negative connotation of the word 'turn,' which I reasoned was a result of idiomatic conditioning in the English language, for example the phrases: 'wrong turn,' 'turn for the worse,' 'turn back,' 'turn off' or 'turn away,' not to mention 'turn up,' which many do dead. And of course 'turn' as in 'rot' or 'go bad.' Thus the word 'turn' is associated with negative idiomances, each of which attributes to a generalized aversion toward the word, even when it's used neutrally or out of context. This idea, by now, that words develop 'feelings' due to repeated usage in particular phraseologies is widely accepted. But at the time of my dissertation it was somewhat fringe stuff. I published my thesis, as you may know, as a book titled *A Turn of Phrase*."

"I . . . haven't read it. Sorry."

"And here I am. Turning right and left and right and then right again and left and right and left twice and right and left and right and left and left and left and right, right, right, left, right, left, left, right, left, right, left, right, left, right, right, right, right and left. Or at least I think that's the order. Maybe it was left, right, right, left, right, left, left, right, left, left, right, left, right, left, right, right, right, left and left."

X Parke shrugs at the gate. "Who can say?"

"Who *can* say? Though I suspect that a good life is not one in which the walls of life are cleared, but rather one in which a route between the walls is memorized. And in this way I have come to live a bad life."

"I really need to keep going. I'll send help I promise."

"I'm going to die in here," Harold whispers. "I'm going to die in this maze and never be found. My wife will think I've abandoned her. My children will not remember me. I'll be spoken about with derision—if I'm spoken about at all. I never should have come in here. I had a bad feeling before I ever left my room. I should have gone to the pool. Or sat with a book by the fireplace."

X Parke cranes her neck at a squawk from the sky and feels the weight of her hair tug the taut skin of her scalp, and the water in the plastic gallon sloshes as if she'd shifted more dramatically than she thinks she did. There'd been an incident in high school where a student had made various death threats against a teacher and a group of students, and had been expelled, and for weeks after the expulsion X Parke remembers people—her included—walking anxiously through the halls, making off-color jokes to offset the fear that this student would show up and carry out his threats, though he never did.

"They'll say that I *wanted* to be in here," Harold's voice continues. "That I *chose* to remain inside the maze. That I did this on purpose. And who can blame them for saying that? If I heard about me, Professor Harold William Blyzniak, published author, avid bicyclist, husband father son brother, I too would know not what to make of it other than to assume he'd made a choice, that he'd traded his life and life's objects to walk in circles through a roughly thirty-foot-by-thirty-foot hedge maze. Why else would he die inside? Because he'd gotten *lost*? I think not."

"Maybe you can leave a trail," X Parke sighs. "Like . . . like that guy in the myths. Or Hansel and Gretel. If you have something, coins or something. That way you'll know if you've already been one way and you can cross it off and try a different way."

A beat of silence. ". . . Are you a child?"

"I'm . . . No. I'm eighteen."

"Please, go fetch an adult. Go fetch the oldest person you can find and tell them I'm in here, that I need help. Please. The older the better."

"I *am* an adult . . ." X Parke entwines her fingers.

"I won't argue with you, Rose," Harold's voice hardens. "I refuse to argue with you further. If you say you are grown enough to go, then go. But remember that to be grown is to take ownership over your own suffering. I will not abide a 'talk' years from now in which you accuse me of failing to parent you, or blame me for your conditions. Be grown, then, and sleep in your own bed. So to speak."

"I'll get help," X Parke steps away from the gate. "As soon as I can."

"They'll say: 'Harold Blyzniak gave up, sequestered himself to a self-imposed exile from the demands of his adulthood. An atavistic slump. A reverse Philitas of Cos. What a waste. What a failure."

"I'm leaving . . ."

"Or they'll say he was demented. As in with dementia. Or early onset Alzheimer's. Or that he'd been uncareful and suffered some sort of catastrophic brain injury. Or worse they'll say that he *wanted* to be in here. That he *chose* to wander inside a maze. That he did this on purpose. And who can blame them for saying that? If I heard about me, Professor Harold Willhelm Blyzniak, published author, avid bicyclist, husband father son, I too would assume he'd made a choice, that he'd traded his life and life's obligations to walk in circles through a roughly thirty-foot-by-thirty-foot hedge maze. Why else would he die inside? Because he'd gotten *lost*? Adults do not get lost in mazes . . ."

X Parke sidles from the gate.

"They'll likely also say he got lost and perished in a *labyrinth*. People always make that mistake. Most won't know the difference, but those who do will think Harold Blyzniak was a fool. Mentally ill. To get lost in a labyrinth . . . It would be harder to get lost in a labyrinth than not, assuming you don't stop walking or change direction. The Hopi have stories of I'itoi, a mischievous god who resides in a cave beneath the Boboquivari Mountains known colloquially as 'The Man in the Maze.' But it's often represented as an image of a figure standing at the mouth of a labyrinth. The allegory is one pertaining to the *perceived* intricacies of life against the imminence of death and inevitable removal from the labyrinth. In this case the labyrinth being life. Though from in here I appreciate that life is riddled with true puzzles, choice and chance, every moment a maze. And yet of course there is no real choice, since we all end up at the same place eventually."

X Parke starts up the valley.

"People correlate option with solution, mistakenly inferring that a corridor with more offshoots is more likely to reach an end. Or that *those* offshoots will yield a greater degree of further offshoots and therefore potential solution etcetera etcetera. This implies a misled correlation between 'option' and 'solution.' Of course if the goal is to escape the maze, then necessarily all maze agents must incorrectly apply this dislogic at least *twice*, so the maze can be entered in the first place."

X Parke waves at no one.

"Therefore *en limnis*—'in the marsh'—or in 'the maze of tombs.'" Harold's voice rises. "Egyptians built maze complexes around the sarcophagi of their pharaohs to keep people out or to keep the pharaohs in. Like Skotino Cave and Gortyn. Procrustes of the Standard Bed. Jack Torrance in the film. Or the 'Chakravyuha' in the *Mahabhranta*. Churned through the gut of the monster. Digested like food. *Hic inclusus, vitam perdit. In girum imus nocte et consumimur igni* . . . . We go wandering at night, Rose, and are consumed by fire . . ."

8

The valley progresses and narrows into a ravine along the nadir of which X Parke's walking now, its crests lined with spinous trees on either side and plantless along its walls where it's too steep for snow and loose red dirt gleams and hardens as she goes into rock. There's a bird trilling eagerly or frantically overhead, and footsteps clucking toward her from the north, but each time she stops to listen they vanish. Occasionally, dark cavities in the red rock wall from which trees or boulders may have been wrested and which remind X Parke of the dark cavities left by pulled teeth, which come to think of it she's not sure she's actually ever *seen* but of which she has a pretty solid image in her head nonetheless. Back in September there'd been a hurricane elsewhere, a bad one that battered the seaboard. X Parke and the Jessas had pored over photos in the news of people stranded on rooftops, storefronts cracked open and plundered, drowned dogs arranged along strips of tarp. There was one picture that really stuck with them: a rocky beach strewn with whale carcasses, faceless, their withered skin lacerated with white scars that seemed to spell out desperate, clandestine phrases. The roommate Jessa had painted this image in her art class and hung it over her bed. X Parke didn't mind the morbidity—there was something beautiful about the faultlessness in the whales' deaths—but found the painting's shoddy craftsmanship highly offensive. Luckily, it was only up until the first week of November, when a particularly raucous night of Hammond's and boys had torn it off the wall. Jessa threatened to redo it, but by then the hurricane and its dead whales had staled into the past, and any effort to memorialize the event would have appeared as genuine mournfulness rather than dark irony, the former of which Jessa was incapable of and the latter for which there were endless further opportunities. And lo by semester's end a new Jessa original was hung there, this one of an emaciated old woman on a hospital bed with the sheets bunched away from her papery legs and her eyes gawping and her hands clawed, a gathering of faceless family to one side. Death's not really sad to X Parke because the fact that life exists—that anything exists at all—is just so completely unpromised. Not that. Stupefying. Divine. None of those, something there's no word for. So why should something that's a built-in part of this divinely stupefyingly unpromised thing be sad? Sad is pretty selfish, X Parke thinks, tracing a faded shape on the red rock wall that might just barely be a stick figure drawing, though headless. And shortsighted. When X Parke's grandpa'd died her junior year of high school, her dad's dad, she'd felt something, but it was muted, sepia. She was blasé. Not because she didn't love her grandpa, but because she didn't understand what everyone else expected to happen. That he would just somehow dodge the one thing that absolutely happens to everybody else? How can the singular unifying experience of all life be sad? If you died that means you lived, and that should be enough. That should be good. Or is X Parke too young, as she suspects, to accommodate these dueling conditions in her underdeveloped brain? Something can be good and sad at the same time, X Parke understands but doesn't feel. It feels like it's got to be one or the other, or some third condition for which she has neither the emotional nor intellectual capacity. Nor the language.

Also she didn't really know her grandpa well, and of course doesn't remember anything about him from before she was twelve or thirteen.

The ravine's wall now crowded with faded drawings, X Parke standing back to look and make sense of them and deducing the following figures in order from left to right: a huddle of headless stick figures around a thuck of chalk or whatever that might be a small fire; the stick figures in a line behind the fire, or in front of it depending on which way they're facing which, without heads—or even if they did have heads but no faces—is impossible to discern; the same line of stick figures, only now there is one less, and the one directly next to the fire is larger than before, twice as large; again the figures in a line, and again one less figure, and again the first one's larger, has tripled in size; this progresses, the figures disappearing one by one and the one by the fire multiplying in size until it's gigantic and alone beside the fire; now the fire growing and changing, elongating into a pillar of smoke or a house until it's taller than the single gigantic headless figure and the figure leaning head-first into the smoke or house and disappearing and the smoke or house shrinking back into a small fire; the fire alone; the fire; just the fire ad nauseam until the ravine curves rudely away. X Parke stretches her arms over her head and cranes her toes upward and exhales a line of breath toward the sky. For some reason she's reminded of the time in high school that her class had gone to an apple orchard one autumn to watch some guy churn butter in a wooden vat and darn a sock, which was exactly as tedious as it sounds, and X Parke and the non-boyfriend whose name she can't remember had slipped away and walked along the corridors of apple trees without talking much and X Parke having to remind the non-boyfriend thrice not to eat the apples that were on the ground because if they'd fallen on their own that meant something was wrong with them, and they'd snaked their way through the orchard thus and saw a youngish couple pushing a girl in a wheelchair over the rutted ground, the girl's face hitched upward, her lips pursed and raised and her eyes rolled back, her wrists hooked and her fingers curled and her feet, too, flexed toward her shins so the entire crux of her body seemed to thrust up toward the sky. And X Parke'd waved and said hi as they passed and the couple'd ignored her or genuinely hadn't noticed her and pushed the wheelchair onward, jostling it in a deep trench and disappearing among the orchard's twisted trunks, and as X Parke and the non-boyfriend walked onward X Parke thought the non-boyfriend was humming to himself, though then she realized that it wasn't him humming, but someone else, from elsewhere in the orchard. And X Parke remembers feeling bad for the girl in the wheelchair, bad that she was stuck where she was, and how she was, and sad that the girl's agency was challenged, or that she had no agency at all, because this, to X Parke, is a thing that's sadder than dying, is being alive without will or without the equipment to act on that will, and the girl in the wheelchair with her whole self permanently locked upward as if trying to get out of the body's prison and soar, was the epitome of tragedy, curling up at the sky, to X Parke, though maybe she has it wrong.

The ravine narrows further so X Parke needs to turn and sidle between the ravine's walls and hold the plastic gallon of water over her head where the ravine flares slightly in order to get it through. The strip of ground here is spotchily snow-covered and damp, and X Parke breathes deep the rich odor of the soil and wants it to remind her of something, though it doesn't, and she grimaces with frustration that the world is not doing what she wants it to do for her, which is a familiar feeling, feeling ensnared in the gears of a world that does not move for her, and she remembers going on just one occasion to the non-boyfriend's house after school, and sitting in his den with the earphones fastening their brains together—remembers for some reason thinking about or focused on the empty sockets of their opposing ears—and there being a knock on the door of the non-boyfriend's house, which the non-boyfriend ignored and X Parke'd heard his mom trot down the stairs and open the front door and then muted voices eking through the house and into the den, though she couldn't make them out, and X Parke'd asked the non-boyfriend who was here, who his mom was talking to, and the non-boyfriend'd said, "My dad," and X Parke'd nodded and pursed her lips because the non-boyfriend's parents were divorced, which was something X Parke knew about but didn't understand and which had the curious effect of making the non-boyfriend's house feel senile and prolix with too much furniture serving too little purpose, this divorced house, and X Parke'd asked, "What are they talking about?" and the non-boyfriend'd said, "I'll tell you later," though he never did, and for some reason X Parke felt a good deal of foreboding surrounding the exchange, austerity in the non-boyfriend's voice and the sort of base dirtiness she associated with divorce and its very dingy and adult connotations, and she imagined for some reason that in retrospect eludes her that the non-boyfriend's divorced parents were out on the front porch examining each others' genitals, again for whatever reason, and not in a sensual way but rather in this very mechanical, rote and obligatory way as if they were compelled to do so by order of some judge or something, an exercise conditional on remaining divorced as punishment for having been reckless enough to marry in the first place. And now of course X Parke knows that nothing like this was going on on the front porch, that the non-boyfriend's parents were just talking, and that the foreboding austerity in the non-boyfriend's voice when he'd said, "I'll tell you later," was not alluding to any kind of grave revelation but rather betraying that he didn't know the answer. He didn't know what his parents were doing on the porch, what they were talking about, and this not knowing frustrated him and in his teenage mind he couldn't formulate this frustration as a shareable expression and so employed the ominous "I'll tell you later" by way of off-putting all of this frustration about not knowing and feeling shut out from the vast and arduous and ostensibly unending land of acquiescing to not knowing, which is a very grownup land which X Parke thinks *should* be off-limits to children since they have enough to deal with insofar as the myriad troubling ways children suffer through the delirium of their half-formed consciousnesses to begin with. Which brings X Parke again to her memory problem, and she wonders if more than her memory has been depredated, if something pertaining to her development out of or away from childhood has suffered, and she feels, as the ravine tightens, stillborn, and abject—though these terms seem disparate and out of context, though in this moment 'context' and 'disparateness' are things X Parke's not so sure about. Ablated is how she feels, or atrophied. There's a Lenape word, *niski*, which X Parke learned from reading Blythe, meaning 'dirty,' though not as in 'covered in dirt' but rather as in 'corrupt' or else otherwise qualitatively base, which is getting closer to how X Parke feels, needing to turn her feet outward and do this crab-like shuffle through the ravine-cum-crevice, though 'feels' maybe also isn't right, because 'feelings' are ephemeral, and herd along and bleed away like clouds. 'States' and 'conditions' are the sky behind, as permanent as anything—though, like 'context,' 'permanence' is something X Parke's suddenly not so sure about.

Now just as the crevice constricts to the point where X Parke's unable to get a full breath from the rock depressing her diaphragm—finding some amusement here over the regularly somewhat good-natured hard time the Jessas gave her about her skinniness, which here is permitting her, barely, passage through this crevice which of course neither Jessa would've made it through with their otherwise useful boobs and butts—the crevice gives abruptly onto the woods and X Parke squeezes out and breathes and brushes at her hoodie from which tufts of red dust and webby tendrils detach and float off. Looking back at the narrow fissure out of which she's just popped—and she's amazed she fit out at all because from here it's just barely a slit in the rock—there's a block of ice protruding from the rock's base near the fissure that's melting oddly so ramous pathways bore through its bulk, X Parke suspicious there might be a pattern in the ice though obviously there isn't and the pathways are mere ramifications of a mindless nature disinterested in signaling anything to X Parke at all or to anyone, which reminds her of getting high that one time in the shallow woods behind campus with the Jessas and on account of some quality of that particular bag of weed or just some other nebulous conditions of the day they'd all three grown paranoid and squirrely and kept hearing things—twigs snapping and/or rustling and/or the nasally cadence of human voices—from nearby and at one point one of the Jessas had yelped and run off into the woods in the opposite direction of campus and X Parke and the remaining Jessa had looked panicked at one another and run after her and run blindly swatting at branches and bramble not knowing what they were running from but so utterly determined in that instant to flee that they didn't even realize they were running into a tangle of briars until they'd gotten sufficiently hooked and barbed and grinded to a halt and eventually suspended there off the ground by their clothes in this lake of briars all at some distances from one another and panting and terrified and X Parke'd yelled at the Jessa who'd run first to explain what she'd run from and she'd stammered and said that she'd just meant it as a prank, like just to scare them, and the other Jessa'd cursed and thrashed against the briar which only further ensnared her and X Parke'd merely shook her head at the sky which is the direction in which the briar'd happened to face her and the three had literally hung around the briar patch the rest of the afternoon not speaking until some boys happened to walk nearby and spotted them and one had a knife which he used to saw them free and besides for some superficial scratches the girls were unscathed and'd ended up hanging with the boys who'd freed them, who were a couple years older and nerdy-cool, and later that night they'd all even laughed about the stupid incident genuinely but they never bought weed again from the person they'd bought that weed from and moving forward did most of their smoking indoors, in the dorm. The exception being the time they'd gone to the reservoir in October right as autumn was peaking and the trees around the water silently burning bouquets of gold and purple and this time the weed'd calmed them and made them even pensive and they'd spoken out at the water about little things that X Parke doesn't even remember now, though she does remember the doe that loped into view at the reservoir's edge, pausing not far from them and craning down to lap at the still water, the ripples, one Jessa choosing that moment to skip a rock, which startled the doe and sent her retreating through the tree line, and X Parke remembers also the brace of sparrows bickering in the white sky, and the roar of a truck's engine faraway, and the codes of moss draped across the stone pier on which the girls stood looking out, X Parke commenting on the water and how cold it must be, and a Jessa shouting something incoherent and leaping from the pier with her clothes and everything, and the other Jessa following and the two Jessas treading and beckoning to X Parke, who teetered incredulously on the pier's edge, turning in circles and pawing at her hair, wondering then if this was a moment she'd remember perfectly forever or if she'd forget it entirely like she had her childhood, and finally jumping as a fan of leaves carved toward the reservoir's surface, and deciding that the truth, like in all cases, was going to land somewhere in the middle.

9

Soon through the base of a glassy hill of packed ice cuts a rill of blue water, X Parke now kneeling and dumping the sludgy snow-water from the plastic gallon and refilling it with this purer blue water. The sun's location is not obvious, whereas through the branches' gaps there's gray now, and the air is dampened and still. Then where the trees spread back around an unblemished white meadow X Parke stops at its edge and upturns her face to find a silence of geese scoring high through the low sky in a formation approximating the letter M or H depending on the parallax, and she recognizes the geese, or thinks she could recognize them, or has déjà vu or something—it's not obvious here what happens at the edge of the meadow but ultimately X Parke clocks the bulging gray sky and its implications and hurries into the meadow toward the opposite tree line with arms tucked down at waist and the hood of her hoodie kind of . . . again it's not obvious what is notable about her hood, or even exactly where she is in the meadow now at all. The geese a black line segment over the trees, seeming stuck there and suspended as the snow-clouds cow the meadow and the first fat snowflakes spill onto the meadow's outspread snow where a set of footprints pivot right and left and spiral, hesitate and churn the snow into an oblate shape then slope east to north again and disappear and reappear elsewhere looping and dotting, and I am struck by something about the word 'footprint' being tricky insofar as the actual object 'footprint' is contingent on there being another thing for in which the print to manifest, in other words and not only that but a 'footprint''s the displacement of another thing and not its own thing altogether, meaning a 'footprint' cannot exist independently of or from a thing qualified by its nature to receive or transmit a footprint, depending how you look at it. And yet this negative space, a footprint, is an indicator of being. And I start to interrogate the autonomy of other objects relative to their positions, as in take any tree here around the meadow, any tree whose treeness is dependent on the anti-treeness of its surroundings, whereas if all the trees were 'tree' then no tree could be 'tree' but only the *footprint* in the 'tree' or if the sky was 'tree' along with the trees then would there be both sky and tree, or neither? Or would there be something else entirely? And how many boundaries can be struck back before there is only one thing? And here from the empty meadow's midpoint I am at once relieved of my delusion and accede that there *is* only one thing, one thing with no size, shape or aspect and which is spatially and temporally homologous, and that description inflicts parameters and draws the thing into discrete parts—parts being described parameters of the thing—and that actuality is a composite of parts; furthermore the thing cannot be described in its own terms, and that what cannot be described cannot be encountered, meaning therefore we have no relationship with the thing other than to name a postulation of its entirety; in other words: the thing is whatever is not described, and neither diminishes nor augments when a part is described, being not made of parts, but homologous, and impervious to quantification whereas infinite parts could be described from it, the thing acquiescing infinite parts because infinite descriptions can be given, and no matter how many parts are described, the potential for the creation of subsequent parts is unlimited; parts being any described parameter that differs from another, whereas the parameter of a part is as it has been described and is not intrinsic to the part because the part is separate from the thing only insofar as it has been described to be (i.e. 'footprint' from 'meadow' or 'snow'), nor is a part intrinsically dimensional but rather inherits its dimension through a description of its parameters, and in the same vein, a part is not intrinsically as it is described: changing the description of a part will alter a part's parameter given that a part has no innate properties because describing a part is representational rather than interpretational—it is parameter *giving* rather than parameter *finding*—and to describe a part is to draw its parameter, which parameter is only as dimensional as the language of its description, and if a parameter is only as dimensional as its description, and a part is only as dimensional as its parameter, then a part and its description are inextricable: parts are made of their descriptions, meaning if a description cannot be given, there is no part, in other words description is concurrent with the creation of a part, and a part does not exist without a description of its parameter, so to be described is to be a part and to be a part is to be described; whereas further a part can only be described comparative to the description of other parts and parts differ from one another only insofar as they are described to differ, since the thing has no aspect against which to contrast the description of a part, and thus there can never be just one part but there must exist at least two parts for there to exist any part at all, and that once described a part must be separate from the thing and is irrevocable to the thing: it enters our actuality, which is to say that how we describe parts is how actuality is, and that our relationship with actuality—a composite of all the parts—is contingent on our ability to describe it, so therefore that which we cannot describe we do not experience, and thus the nature of actuality is determined by the conditions set by the descriptions of the parts that comprise it. The thing is all that *must* exist. The thing must exist regardless of the naming of it. This makes it the only *truth*. Parts are *not true* in that no part or any part must exist and no description of any part's parameter is perdurable. A footprint is only distinct from a meadow because I've named its parameters. The creation of parts is arbitrary and parts are not intrinsically related and the drawing of any one part does not allow us to infer whether any other part is drawn or not, because the relationship between parts is inherited through the reticulum of the language used to draw the parameter of a part. Decision is the principle of description: Where does one part end and another begin? As parts are described, descriptions of subsequent parts respond to preexisting parameters. The same way the eye does not make the object it observes and the object does not make its observance in the eye, neither does description precede itself in manifesting the parameters it describes. Description and actualization are mimetic processes—when they come together they produce the illusion of fact and form. And here finally X Parke reappears on the meadow's far side, her hood down and a single white hair lain behind her ear starkly contrasting the predominant black, and X Parke is feeling as if something of some import has transpired, though in then attempting to identify it finds nothing of note, just a traipse through a normal meadow with no special qualities or characteristics, and she pushes onward into the forest, coming soon to the crest of a gully where stout rocks like effigies at its bottom gather what meager snow manages to wrest its way through the forest's canopy, X Parke pausing here at the gully's crest to cast a sidelong scowl downward—as a green pewee pitches from a bough to the ground, skitters beneath the icy brush—before drawing her hood back up around her grave face and trudging northward again.

10

The thing about T or Bad Stuff as Malory'd called it that X Parke's considering now as the forest thickens and occasional angles of rusted metal stab up through the pitted snow that must be debris from an old car wreck or something similar X Parke figures is that the detriment inherent in T or BS is only apparent afterward and never during, especially in X Parke's case which is especially this way given that she doesn't remember any explicit T or BS or even know for sure if there even was any T or BS at all to begin with but is certain that something detrimental is going on now and that everything that goes on goes on for a reason. In other words it's probably hard or impossible to say for certain whether something that's happening which you're in the midst of does or does not constitute T or BS whereas down the line and from the vantage of hours or days or many many years you can be certain about the T-tic nature of that something and can make a claim about the de facto detriment of the BS and even measure that detriment maybe somehow and quantify it. X Parke now avoiding a jagged sheet of aluminum or tin and starting to tally the detriment that may or may not result from a possible T or some BS in the years before twelve or thirteen, the first thing that's coming to mind being obviously the absence of memory from before twelve or thirteen altogether. Another possible detriment or definite detriment that's possibly resultant from some ostensible T or BS is the social awkwardness. It's not something X Parke had considered abnormal or an issue really at all until the Jessas made an issue out of it and forced her to consider it. In high school X Parke'd just been a weird and quiet girl, but in college, at the authority of the Jessas, X Parke'd been diagnosed socially awkward. For her on the inside, it's maybe best describable as timidity she thinks, as in feeling timid and uncertain about whether the angle of her face relative to other people is befitting and/or what to do with her hands and/or mouth when they're not in use. But on the outside apparently, according to the Jessas, it's this kind of cumbrous disposition involving inappropriate levels of eye contact—either too much or too little depending on the circumstance—and weird body positioning whereas she's always facing someone too much or not enough—again depending—and this thing she does with her lips where it looks like she's chewing when there's demonstrably no food around and not to mention the finger entwining which the Jessas *really* hate because they say it makes it look like X Parke has more fingers than she should and all this is probably in large part, according to the Jessas, the reason X Parke's never had a real boyfriend. Despite that X Parke considers the Jessas somewhat stupid about a lot of things—like neither'd ever heard of in vitro fertilization for example or knew that that was possible—they are undeniably smart about other things, for example about how X Parke comes across to other people, which they of course have a better grasp of from their external vantage than X Parke does from her interior one. But however their evaluation of the ways in which X Parke is awkward is helpful merely on a cosmetic level and does nothing insofar as deciphering a solution to the underlying causes of said awkwardness. This X Parke understands—as she pauses briefly and for no good reason traces the dull edge of a twisted piece of rust protruding from the snow like a shark's fin and then sniffs her fingers which smell, naturally, ferric—is *her* job.

Though it should be noted that both Jessas have confessed to X Parke on various occasions their own Ts and BS. One of them described one night after a few Hammond's Hard Ciders and a spliff or two and in what X Parke found to be very exacting and yet peripheral detail her T-tic BS as it occurred at sleepaway camp, Camp Kwelantamen, when she was ten. The abridged version is that she was heading back to her bunk one evening after dinner and by herself for some reason which she made a note to note was unusual and but while taking a shortcut from the campground's main lawn—which is where the mess hall and the administrative buildings were clustered—through a shallow copse along the lake's perimeter to get a sweater from her bunk before that evening's evening activity, she'd heard a sound like a whimper from deeper off in the copse and had stopped to look, and this was in July and it was only 6pm or 7pm and so still pretty much completely light out and yet the section of trees from which she'd heard the whimper was sort of gnarled in shadow on account of just the way the trees there were positioned, and she'd really needed to squint and peer which as she did she discerned a group of people, older boys who were actually junior counselors Jessa was pretty sure, standing in a circle facing one another there in the thicker part of the lake's perimeter's shallow copse, and at first she couldn't tell what they were doing but then saw someone else there sitting on the ground in their midst, a little boy, and recognized him as the younger brother of one of her best camp friends, a boy named Theo who had Asperger's and was part of the sleepaway camp's daycamp program which ran usually from 8 a.m. to 8 p.m. and now here he was whimpering on the ground surrounded by these much older junior counselors and at first Jessa figured that he'd hurt himself somehow or gotten lost, "since kids with Asperger's can get lost and hurt themselves at a higher rate than kids without Asperger's," and that the junior counselors were gathering there to help him. But then as she watched on she saw that one of the junior counselors had his dick out and was peeing on Theo, right on his head, and in fact so was another of the junior counselors, and as Jessa watched another one took out his dick too and started peeing and all the while Theo's whimpering and his fists are dug into the mulchy ground and the junior counselors are snickering very quietly, which signaled to Jessa that they knew what they were doing was wrong and so were trying not to draw attention to themselves because why else would they be being so quiet if they weren't trying to conceal something and anyway Jessa hurried on to her bunk and got a sweater and took the path back, which curled the long way around the copse, to the campground's main lawn and met up with her friends including her friend who was the older sister of Theo and the worst part Jessa said is that she didn't say anything to anyone about it for some reason and acted like nothing'd happened and joined the other campers at the fire pit where as the sun set down behind them purpling Lake Kwelantamen they all listened to a scary story told by none other than one of the junior counselors she'd seen peeing on Theo about a monster called the Doughboy which was a traditional camp tale around here and involved a misshapen creature that lurked along the boulders at the foothills of the Wipid Mountains—which towered over the campgrounds to the northwest—who had allegedly once been a camper but through a series of ever-changing conditions was condemned for eternity to scramble through the boulders eating other campers since apparently other campers were the only things that sated the Doughboy's infinite hunger and Jessa didn't see Theo again that night though she saw him the next day when his mom dropped him off and he seemed his usual withdrawn and messy-haired self except perhaps a little more withdrawn and messy-haired than usual and at one point that day or the next day he'd come up to his sister who was hanging out with Jessa and the other girls on the lawn near the tetherball court and tried to hug her and she'd pushed him away and called him a retard and laughed and the other girls had laughed and Jessa'd laughed too.

To this the other Jessa had rolled her eyes and asked how any of that constituted T—though she'd used of course the actual word—given that none of it had actually happened *to* her but rather just *around* her and actually if anything she'd ultimately contributed to Theo's T by not taking any action to help or protect him and if she wants to feel bad about anything then she should feel bad about that. X Parke then commenting that T can manifest for different people in different ways, and it's not anyone else's responsibility to take inventory of someone else's T because what does and does not constitute T and its outcomes vary from person to person like for example some people may become awkward and lose their memories. The other Jessa then again rolling her eyes and saying "I've got some T for you," and proceeding to tell her own story about the T of her father's suicide when she was seven, her father having shot himself in the den with Jessa and her mom in the house and without leaving a note or anything and so utterly out of nowhere that for years Jessa's mom was convinced he'd been murdered somehow because why would a man with no history of depression or any financial problems or health issues and a beautiful family do something like this? Though the police investigated and investigated and forensics showed that he'd 99% shot himself and it couldn't be any other way and even to this day Jessa's mom is suspicious that something's been left undetermined or unexamined and in other words something's not right. But the father's suicide was a long time ago and Jessa's mom's since gotten remarried to Jessa's stepdad who's a decent man even though he does this thing where he scolds his two Rottweilers when they're going to the bathroom even when they're going to the bathroom outside so that they get scared and confused and don't know where to poop, and then the stepdad laughs and says stuff like "Stupid dogs" or "That was too easy" as if he's doing something really clever by getting one over on these poor animals who don't want anything in the world other than to make him happy though besides that charming personality trait he's a decent man though once when she was fifteen Jessa'd gotten out of the shower and was toweling off in the bathroom and he'd come right in and stopped in the doorway looking at her for a full couple seconds before saying "Oops, sorry" and backing out and shutting the door and at first Jessa didn't think anything of it though later upon reflection she remembered that he'd been coming down the hall when she'd gone *into* the bathroom to shower and had absolutely clocked her there and she was suspicious now that he'd come in on purpose to get an eyeful of her naked body. "Though the whole walking-in-on-me-in-the-bathroom thing didn't bother me that much," Jessa said lighting a fresh spliff and wobbling her Hammond's, "because like so what if he wants to see me naked who can blame him? And it's not like he ever touched me or ever said anything inappropriate to me and I don't feel threatened by him at all I feel worse for his dogs. And anyway it's my dad's suicide which's the [T]. Not the stepdad stuff. And I saw my dad dead with his head open when I was seven and so what if my stepdad saw me in the bathroom with my clothes off when I was fifteen?"

Meanwhile now X Parke navigating a field of icy knee-high boulders that spill from the suddenly exhausted forest and gather and grow toward the base of a lone treeless hill rounded somewhat too perfectly there directly to the north and thus blocking her path. The sky's doing this thing where there's still snow ashing down from a clot of flaky clouds to the west but then the sky's clear to the north and east and on account of the clouds' contrast is shockingly blue and rich and X Parke thinks about Malory and hopes he isn't mad that she left without saying goodbye after he'd taken her in like that and they'd spent the night together snuggling with their clothes off and on top of this he'd been so understanding and cool with her not wanting to do anything penetrative and most importantly had really opened up to her about himself and been vulnerable which X Parke found incredibly endearing and flattering and but maybe if she's being honest just a little unattractive though everything else about him was attractive and so one unattractive thing doesn't really tilt the scales as it were though this whole train of thought is moot given that she left without saying goodbye and will never see him again. The lone hill's base by X Parke's estimation is a mile wide or so—though she doesn't have a ton of experience approximating the size of geological formations and it could be three miles or a hundred feet for all she knows, though, again, this is moot given that either way she's not going to climb it and starts picking her way east along the boulders which are big enough now that the fissures between them are deeper than she is tall and she steps cautiously from one to the next and sometimes goes on her knees and sort of planks across especially harrowing fissures because were she to fall into one out here and become stuck then she would die like that for sure. "That would be a nasty exit," X Parke says to the boulders and the hill and the dandruffy snow sliding harmlessly from her hair and hoodie like sand off glass. Soon she's far enough east that she can see around the hill's eastern edge and there's another hill there, identically rounded and treeless and perhaps just slightly larger, and now continuing carefully along the craggy boulders she sees a third hill behind that one, and then a fourth and fifth and so on, all running in an eerily straight line north and increasing slightly in size. She files the Jessas' respective Ts into two columns and lists inside each column the Ts respective T-tizing characteristics by way of determining which is more tragic. Of course the obvious answer is that the dad's suicide is more tragic, since death is always supposed to be more tragic than living in any way. Though and here X Parke furrows her lips at the difficulty of this next thought: there's something about an adult man's suicide that just isn't as tragic as maybe an adult man would want it to be. X Parke now doing a kind of semi-split across a fissure and casting away the remainder of that previous thought, conceding that of course the tragedy is not the dad's suicide as it pertains to the dad, but the finding of the dead dad by the seven-year-old Jessa and her mom and the subsequent lifetime of fatherlessness. The other Jessa's T of course is a different kind, a kind of collateral T or surrogate T that X Parke struggles to describe the parameters of for her column but which she decides has something to do with the tragedy of agency or the lack of agency and which relates to what she'd thought about earlier with the girl in the wheelchair in the orchard, and now in the case of this Jessa's story as it pertains to Theo's age and the Asperger's and also to some extent young Jessa who despite the other Jessa's opprobrium was too young to reasonably absorb culpability for her inaction, who just didn't know better and, alas, ignorance = a lack of agency = tragedy. Here X Parke pausing atop a widthy boulder to catch her breath and plan the continuation of her route and nodding gravely at this not-new idea in re: the lack of agency as key in the potency of tragedy. She wishes she'd mentioned this very important-feeling idea during Prof Lane's class's discussion of *The Long Pig* and Joseph Shapiro's alcoholism and how this alcoholism, which in Joseph's case stripped so much of his agency and autonomy and rendered him incapable of advocating for himself, contributed to the novel's tragic gut-punch of a narrative. This is something Prof Lane would have loved, or maybe not *loved* but admired and would have drawn columns about and lauded X Parke for introducing to the class. But alas. And now X Parke's making her way along the eastern feet of the spinal-columning hills where the boulders persist. And but back to her initial endeavor, she decides the Jessa whose dad killed himself suffered the more tragic T because it was or is tied to some definite problematic stuff with her stepdad which regardless of her insistence that said stuff wasn't T-tizing it is not lost on X Parke that the inclusion of the stepdad in the testimony about the dad's suicide, T-tizing or not, attaches it to the T of the dad's suicide and sets it in accordance with the T because if it really was nothing, like she claimed, then she wouldn't even have mentioned it at all.

Which brings her back to the earlier thought about how T or Bad Stuff is hard to determine as such as it's happening, which is probably what happened to the Jessa whose dad shot himself in the head as it pertains to the stepdad walking-in-on-her-in-the-bathroom incident, which is to say that when it happened, the stepdad, or as it was happening, Jessa was telling herself that it wasn't a big deal and certainly didn't constitute T and sort of concretized that assertion to the extent that now, years later, after the walking-in-on-her has actually manifested as T or Bad Stuff, she's already drawn the parameters of the incident into a permanent non-T and refuses to redraw those parameters and so has no way of addressing the T embedded in the incident other than to lump it into the same cerebration that finding her dead dad inhabits. Proof of T by association. The hills go on and on as far as X Parke can see, and the sky is a smattering. X Parke'd once walked in on the other Jessa, the one who'd said nothing about Theo, with a boy in their dorm room in the middle of a weekday. The door'd been unlocked and there were none of the traditional tokens of occupancy on the door, i.e. a tie or something which in X Parke's and Jessa's case wouldn't have made sense since neither owned a tie but a sock would have sufficed or a scarf or even a bra. Any of those things would have signaled to X Parke that Jessa was getting busy in the dorm room and X Parke would have continued on past the room and gone to the library or the student lounge or whatever and killed an hour. But there was nothing on the dorm's door and because it was the middle of a weekday X Parke's mind never even flirted with the notion that anything un-weekday-like might be unfolding inside. So she'd gone ahead and stepped into the room and shut the door behind her and even dropped her bag on the floor at the foot of her twin bed before noticing Jessa and some boy over on Jessa's side of the room with the boy prostrate on Jessa's twin bed and Jessa crouched over him convulsing it seemed with her face flushed many shades redder than the rest of her pale body and emitting these quiet little eeks like the ones bats make to echolocate, and the boy, who X Parke'd seen around campus but didn't know by name, turned his head and looked directly at X Parke with his mouth curled into this O and his eyes canted in a way that reminded X Parke of the face dogs make when they're pooping, and X Parke was sort of stricken there just watching this, not because it was necessarily shocking on its own—two people having sex was pretty commonplace in college or anywhere—but rather just because she was caught so off-guard and just hadn't expected it, and before she could turn around or shut her eyes or flee from the room, the boy, with his eyes still locked on X Parke, let out this little gasp and his hands scraped along the sheets and his scrawny musculature flexed and Jessa, who still had yet to notice X Parke, starting saying

"Don't cum in me don't cum in me" and the boy, lurching once while still looking directly at X Parke, said "Sorry" and Jessa said "Fuck" and X Parke left and went down the hall to the other Jessa's room but she wasn't there so she went and sat in the quad and listened to a pair of students singing and playing guitars very poorly and when she returned to the dorm room half an hour later the boy was gone and Jessa was on her bed doing homework and didn't even say "Hi" and they didn't talk about anything until that evening when Jessa rolled a spliff and asked if X Parke wanted to hit it, which she did, and then they smoked and talked about Florence, to which Jessa's family had just told her they were all going over the summer, and Jessa kept saying she'd heard about this flash rave in the Colosseum and was gonna have to figure out when it was and how to get invited and X Parke considered not even correcting her but then decided it was an important teaching moment and so went in on her really hard about it to the point that Jessa never even mentioned Florence again for the rest of the semester.

The boulders splintering and moldering to gravel indistinguishable from the ashy snow along the hills' eastern feet, and an aberrant warm wind drives the musk of burning wood. The smell has the sort of anamnestic effect of spiriting X Parke to this past Halloween, when some students had built a bonfire in a field on the campus's outskirts. Prior to going out there, X Parke had been resigned to spend Halloween in her dorm room hacking her way through a section of *The Long Pig* that Prof Lane had insisted was both particularly tricky and particularly important and from which so far X Parke was getting neither. But the Jessas presented to X Parke a counter-option involving dressing up in skimpy shorts and meager tops and thigh-high boots and coloring their hair with this glow-in-the-dark wax they'd procured and then going to the field and candy-flipping. "What's candy-flipping?" X Parke'd asked with her Blythe ramparting the lower half of her face. "It's when you take acid and ecstasy at the same time," said one Jessa or the other, the prospect of which sounded terrifying to X Parke but also weirdly enticing, having taken both before but being unable to begin to wrap her head around the sensory paroxysm that must ensue from both amalgamated. And so it wasn't hard to talk her into it—though she forewent the skimpy shorts and meager tops and thigh-highs although *did* agree to apply a streak of chartreuse to her hair, which looked good enough, as she admired herself in the dorm's bathroom's scuffed mirror, that she considered making it a fulltime thing. Campus was teeming with students and nonstudents and the Jessas enjoyed a glut of attention from the drunken boys caroming in every direction, none of whom even so much as stepped aside for X Parke in her oversized sweater and baggy skinny jeans. At the field there were totems of speakers erected around the bonfire and cranked up enough to compete with their generators' furious roaring and a cacophony of dramatic bass and crass pixie vocals drove the Jessas into an instant convulsive bout of very low-to-the-ground dancing. X Parke meanwhile standing outside the ring of the fire's light as static pattered up the back of her neck and the rolling dark woods beyond the field bubbled and shrank and the distance between her and the bubbling woods opened and X Parke yawned mightily and the word 'YAWN' ballooned from her mouth and fluttered there like a moth and then darted toward the howling bonfire and was swallowed in flame which was at the same instant that X Parke enjoyed a jolt of energy and started forward, and the revelers reveling around the fire, whose shadows guttered from them like smoke, parted as X Parke neared and a passage unfurled to her and the Fire beckoned or else rebuffed her, the music now bleeding the cerebral neons of a coral reef as the Fire bellowed rich consonants and the revelers churned on either side like the gears of an enormous faceless clock, X Parke then kneeling before the Fire with her hands upturned and her face opened to its awesome voice while her knees dug through the cold ground and returned her there, her poor deracinated her, the ground's hospitality and the Fire's prophetic wailing both tonic and tectonic and rattling X Parke at some subterranean level of herself so all the dust there rained from the shelves and the bugs that had been loitering darted elsewhere and X Parke's empty upturned hands were filled with the fragrant berries of the Fire's nictitating branches and she tried to feed herself but the revelers standing angled around her were watching and she did not want them to watch her eat from the Fire so took what it'd given her and backed away to the darker ring of the field as the passage of revelers closed in her wake and blotted the Fire away and muted the Fire's voice to a panicked whisper that X Parke could not discern and when she was safely distant she found the berries were gone and someone must've taken them from her while she was blinking and she cried with her arms at her sides in a way that reminded her of something she couldn't place. And later she'd found herself there in the field with both the Fire and fire gone and the revelers gone and there was no music and it was dark and very cold and the stars were especially distant, X Parke was disoriented and started at first toward the dark glut of woods on the field's wrong side before realizing her mistake and walking back, noticing then the red glow of the campus in the distance and finding a path over which branches hung in chords like the throat of a cadaver, the red glow backlighting the trees and other things festering the rural campus's outskirts as the path curled away and X Parke thought it looked like how she imagined her mind was—red, just out of sight—and managed by this route to return to campus and found it deserted and found her dorm room empty and burrowed herself into her bed, her eyes folded beneath her hair, the trill of birdsong and blips of dropping water in the dark, columns of golden sunlight. A wooded thicket, a temple of human remains: the nave a ribcage, the pulpit a hand presenting a dried heart—the alter—an esophagus the steeple and a brain concealed behind plants and leaves the Object, small dusty figures scurrying in and out, pausing to kneel and worship, chirping a strange dirge, something rustling in the underbrush and the figures scattering and hiding, a white shape rising up, smoke or a small house, and the sound of rumpled paper. X Parke's organs heaving their quiet orchestration now as she follows the spinal hills northward and the sun wavers to her left. She's as much the parts of herself she can see as the parts she cannot. Doesn't her heart continue to beat whether or not she knows it is there? Isn't her blood its own rich color despite her observation? How many secret thoughts hurry through the alleys of her mind against her permission, whispering of revolution? What version would remain without her? Would it be distinguishable? Would it do a better job?

That Halloween had ended with the Jessas blitzkrieging into the room very late or early and exploding the lights on and then collapsing against one another and laughing hysterically at X Parke who they said resembled a deer that'd been struck by a car, and then got busy cracking Hammond's and rolling spliffs and X Parke peered out from her blankets at them and they appeared to be glowing or coruscating as if they were full of fire but as her eyes and mind adjusted she determined rather they were simply drenched in glitter and eventually she got up and drank and smoked with them and together they watched the sky gray through the dorm room's pinched window and the Jessas asked X Parke what had happened to her and she said that she'd just come back here to lie down and that was it and the Jessas told X Parke about their crazy night dancing and then going to a party across campus and getting off with a couple nonstudent-fuckboys and making snow angels in an inflatable pool of glitter and needless to say X Parke's dorm room was infested with glitter for the rest of the semester and likely would be long into a future after she and everyone she knew had died.

It being later noon now with the sun perched just atop the nearest hill's round peak and X Parke's Converse crunching the dry snow and gravel like someone clearing a throat. X Parke's hair oily enough after two-plus days sans showering that it stays in place when she pushes it back from her forehead. When she turns and looks back the treeless hills recede endlessly and shrink to a point; ahead the hills proceed endlessly and grow until the most distant ones are indistinguishable from the gauzy air. To her right a featureless peneplain and darkening curtain of sky. The plastic gallon of water is half and she cradles it in the crook of an arm. She has one-third bag of pretzels remaining and a candy bar in her hoodie's front pocket. She is very small out here compared to the rest of it, and feels that. She's felt it before. Like for example on that night after she'd dropped her final essay off at Prof Lane's office—this being, mind-bogglingly, just three days ago from present—and then had found the Jessas dancing in the quad, which they were wont to do, and X Parke'd danced with them because she was elated at having closed the first eighth of her college career only mildly overwhelmed, and had been enjoying herself and really letting loose with the Jessas, but then the Jessas had taken X Parke suddenly aside and one had said, "There's something we need to do," and X Parke didn't want to do anything because she was having fun dancing for once and was tired too and but was blissed out enough from everything that she'd casually acquiesced and the Jessas had led her from the quad and along the path that ran the campus's circumference with the unlit classroom buildings to the right and to the left the concentrated shadows of the soft mountains that bordered the campus and at their bases the occasional orange rectangle of a house's window. "Where are we going?" X Parke'd asked, unsure about where this path led other than just around the remote northern edge of the campus. The Jessas snickered and locked their arms through hers on either side and in this way escorted her onward until the path veered east along the campus's northernmost edge and the Jessas led X Parke off the path and continued north into the fields of brittle postseason corn there which came all the way up to X Parke's chin in some places and in which she feared there were ticks and lice teeming and but the Jessas seemed unfazed and X Parke'd done her best to just be cool and go with whatever was happening. But soon up ahead a dark shape loomed in the cornfield which X Parke had to identify by only its outline and decided it was one of the many depreciated barns scattered around the college's adjacent landscape, and she'd gotten nervous then mainly because she couldn't imagine for what the Jessas were leading her out to this abandoned barn in the middle of the night, and she'd unclasped her arms from the Jessas' arms and slowed to a stop and said, "What's going on?" and the Jessas had prodded and pushed her onward and said, "There's someone you have to meet," and "Stop being dubious," and X Parke'd scoffed because A) she was impressed to hear a Jessa use this word and especially in this way and B) because she wasn't being dubious at all in simply inquiring about destination/intent and yet the Jessas' defensive reactions caused her to feel dubious and she considered mentioning this irony—a few weeks earlier one of them had needed to write an essay on irony and couldn't really get a head around it and X Parke'd tried to help but couldn't think of an example on the spot and now here was a perfect example though it was weeks too late to be of any use to the essay which, incidentally, was also ironic—but instead in order to rebuff any suspected dubiousness she merely marched on through the cornfield toward the lumbering outline of the barn and the Jessas giggled. And as the barn rose up like smoke ahead X Parke'd begun to feel very small relative not just to it but to the field and to the mountains on the left and to the interminable sky and even to the Jessas and all the other people who she couldn't see but knew were there, and to their lives and the sheer staggering perplexity of their thoughts which though jailed inside the breadbox-sized compartments of their brains were nonetheless more immense in every way that mattered than the endless guttering universe, X Parke then taking each Jessa's hand as they approached the barn and feeling counter-intuitively even more distant from them via contact, feeling distinctly the atoms that made her body turning in their vast, silent world, doing the impossible work of manifesting her shape and holding it together. She was separate from the rest of the universe therefore. And she appreciated this miracle or curse there with the Jessas' hands at some desperate distance from her own and twenty fingers entwined with the dead hairy corn groping at jaw lines and fiddling with clothes' hems and the barn so static that it might be alive. X Parke'd thought then of Joseph Shapiro and the 'unyielding restiveness' of his isolation, specifically the chapter in which he'd gone to the city to 'jailbreak his loneliness' and 'relearn the principles of the thing reified in other people,' only to find, stricken horrified on a crowded corner surrounded by a million people who neither longed for nor acknowledged him, that he was irreparably distinct and irremediably distant from 'the rest of himself,' i.e. other people, and had returned upstate and to his cabin tucked away from the lake and drank until he'd passed out and awoke the next morning to find his dog dead in the kitchen, fixed in an odd position as if she'd been trying to stand but died halfway, her eyes enormous and ossified. He'd rolled her into a sheet and carried her to the front door, then gone around the house gathering her things—her aluminum water bowl, her food dish, the frayed bed she'd slept on for twelve years—and placed them in a box. And when he'd returned to the foyer he'd found the sheet tousled on the floor, checked beneath it, turned in a circle, and the dog'd danced into the foyer and licked his cracked hands, and he'd unpacked her things from the box and given her breakfast. And as the sun dies now behind the white hills and shadows flex across the peneplain, thunder and green lightning macerate the sky to the north, X Parke using the lightning to detect the shape of the distant hills and stay her course, the flat ground steep and her legs knotting, and she yawns and her eyelids harden, and her thoughts wilt and tumble, and she enjoys a series of nebulous ideas which dissolve before she can inventory them, and is left feeling canted back and feet-first, her feet vertical like fence posts and the dark horizon suspended at a gentle arc, the green lightning springing from the arc and posing in the slow, lymphatic sky and then dissolving or not.

11

And as the sun reappears as a gash of red at the peneplain's eastern extremity and purple clouds spew from the gash and stab the still dark western sky where a single star throbs mawkishly at X Parke who's sensing that she recognizes this quadrant of peneplain and this visage of early sky and where the hills were last night there's now a scream of silver mountains and between their feet and X Parke's a stubble of tree stumps and just a little further an abrupt embankment of forest toward which X Parke healthily strides, a sound comes from behind like the scoff of a car's engine, and when she stops and turns to look she sees there in fact, back in the direction from where she's come, a glint of dark metal fast approaching. She considers briefly trying to hide only because she's so surprised by this development rather than genuinely concerned, but the surprise passes and there's nowhere for her to hide—the tree stumps to her left are too low to conceal her—even if she needed to. So she simply stands with her feet together and waits as the car—a black sedan she thinks, though isn't sure from this distance—careers across the peneplain toward her spurting a plumage of ashy dust. X Parke's thinking over and over roughly the words "Finally, someone," as if this car and its occupant(s) is the first life she's encountered since the plane crash, forgetting this is not the case as the car approaches until she remembers Malory all at once and tsks herself for ever having forgotten him—and now remembering also the body on its wires and the brindled face with its deepset black eyes through the limekiln's threshold, and the disembodied voice of Harold Blyzniak, and maybe someone else she's still forgetting—and she attempts to revise the words stuttering through her head to more appropriately reflect the actual circumstance but cannot find a suitable substitute and so continues to think, though more quietly, "Finally, someone."

The car is a black Town Car and is very clean, and it revs toward X Parke so brutally she suspects it does not see her or mind her and she steps up onto a tree stump figuring that if someone were inclined to run her over otherwise they might reconsider if in doing so they would also rend out the bottom of their car. But then just as the car seems doomed to zip by it slows and stops directly here, X Parke blinking now at herself in the mirror-tinted backseat window and floating her hand in front of her nose and mouth to guard from the whorling dust and snow particles whipping obliviously or apathetically onward in the car's previous trajectory. And X Parke cranes forward to see herself disheveled and her eyes sunken from her travails, and though it must be her imagination her hair looks longer and lighter, and for a moment she forgets that she's looking at a window and spreads back her lips to see her teeth, which seem gray in the car, but then is reminded that she's not alone when the backseat window whirrs down and a huge face that's neither X Parke's face nor a human face replaces X Parke's face and breathes through its mouth and X Parke straightens and smoothes her hoodie and a bird darts into the sun.

Then now a voice from the car and a hand guides the dog's enormous head aside and a third face—a human face this time—replaces the dog's at the window and frowns in the car's interior's shadows. "Are you sad, little girl?" it says. And X Parke smoothes her hoodie further and shakes her head no and opens her mouth to speak but then the face speaks again. "I know you," it says, coming forward an inch so that its features resolve in the morning's meek light as it's refracted off the silver mountains to X Parke's back, and X Parke squints more as a gesture of uncertainty than as a method by which to better see and tries to clock the face but cannot though she admits it is vaguely familiar insofar as it's a human face with all the typical human features accounted for. And the face says, "You're X Parke Penate. Reinemarie's daughter. You look just like her."

Here X Parke's shoulders crimp and she snorts and recoils, again more as a signal of surprise than as a genuine gesture, though of course she *is* surprised and shocked to hear her name spoken and her mother's name out here on this peneplain by some face in the backseat of a shiny Town Car, and she says, "How do you know who I am?" though it comes out runneled in whisper and she has to ask again.

The face retreats an inch from the window and the dog's face reappears beside it and dwarfs it and its orange eyes widen. "I've seen your picture," the face nods and the dog nods in conjunction and unfurls a pale tongue. "There used to be pictures of you all over your house, I'm sure you know. You're just as pretty as your mother. In all the same ways."

The sun now cresting the car's roof and bloodying X Parke's eyes in red light.

"I'm on my way to your family's house presently, of all places," says the face. "If you happen to be doing the same, I will gladly carry you the rest of the way."

X Parke recalling now the story she and all of us grew up with wherein blank serendipitous opportunity proves ultimately not so serendipitous for little girl or boy who does not discover the non-serendipity of said blank opportunity until it's too late and said little girl or boy is being fattened up for eating and/or eaten outright. "How do you know my family?" X Parke smoothes her hoodie.

The face wavers in the car's interior's shadow and the dog nods. "It's not a short answer, but if I had to make it short, I'd say I helped with their finances. *Your* finances, plainly. My name is Samuel Grillet, accountant. Perhaps they've mentioned me."

X Parke nods, though she believes she's never heard the name.

"Of course they have," Samuel continues. "We've all become close since they brought me on. A family's money is intimate, as intimate as anything else a family keeps to themselves," his eyes signal briefly behind X Parke, who fights the urge to turn. "And so the decision to bring in an outsider to examine and manage those finances is no casual one, and often I've found I grow close, intimate, with the family whose finances I am brought in to oversee. As is the case with yours. I am intimate with your family, X Parke. Especially your mother."

X Parke continues to nod.

The dog's huge face retreats into the car's interior and Samuel's face swims into the open window and grins at X Parke in a way that X Parke interprets as intending to connote friendliness but which ends up connoting merely an attempt at friendliness which X Parke interprets as indicating a distinct lack of genuine friendliness and she waves her hand near her face as if at a bothersome odor and says, "I appreciate your offer but I think I'll continue on my own." Then adds, "I've made it this far."

Samuel Grillet scoffs. "Nonsense," and prods an instrument-long finger over the window and crooks it at X Parke's Converse. "Those shoes seem ready to dissolve from your feet. And it's cold out there besides. I have heat and a place to sit. What possible excuse could you make to that?"

X Parke grins her own attempt at friendliness and shrugs. "Again I appreciate the offer, but I'm going to say no." And steps off the tree stump and starts north again with the red sunlight painting the right half of her face into a purple wound.

"Your mother said you were wayward," Samuel Grillet chortles as the Town Car pulls up alongside X Parke and matches her pace. "She told me that as a little girl you insisted on everything your way, even when such way spat in the face of ease."

Here X Parke literally stopping midstride. "My mom told you stories about my childhood?"

"Yes. Quite a few."

"What age?"

"Pardon?"

"What age am I in the stories my mom told you."

"Oh I can't say for certain. Certainly no older than eleven or twelve."

X Parke frowns north where the mountain's feet are swarmed with white forest and the sky is a disjunction of morning and night. She experiences a strobe of thoughts that settle, for whatever reason, on Malory's arm around her shoulder and his hand cupping her breast as she kneaded his penis under the blankets in the dead hotel near the dying fire while he mumbled over and over, "I feel you. There's no way. I feel you." And under those blankets X Parke'd thought of Ms. Inoue describing the implacable distance between atoms and the concept that "things never touched," and X Parke'd felt Malory too, in her hand and on her breast and the heat of his breath and even in other less tangible ways she'd felt his longing and his despair and the terrifying solidarity of his being and wondered how on earth none of that constituted touching. And she feels the weight of the plastic gallon of water in her hand and fingers the pretzels and candy bar in her hoodie's front pocket and then touches her own bare forearm with her fingernails—which are longer than she usually keeps them—and breathes through her nose and feels the cold air touch the raw skin inside her nostrils and now shaking her head stops and turns back to the Town Car which also stops and Samuel Grillet's pinched face weaves just inside the backseat window and X Parke says, "Will you tell me some?" and Samuel grins further and says, "Tell you some what?" and X Parke says, "Some of the stories my mom told you about me. Will you tell me some?" and Samuel's face rises and falls and then recedes into the car's interior's shadows and the door clicks and opens and then a moment unfurls in which X Parke is still and the car is still and the sun even seems not to rise just for some seconds until then everything starts up again and X Parke climbs into the Town Car's backseat and closes the door behind her and the sun thrashes up over the peneplain and churns the ashy snow into vapor.

The car's burgundy interior *is* warm, as Samuel claimed, and not only is there a place to sit but *two* places to sit opposite each other, X Parke taking the seat at the car's rear given Samuel's now sitting on the seat across, facing her. His legs are crossed and his hands are folded in his lap and now that X Parke's getting a good look at him she's relieved by his sheer slenderness and the femininity of his disposition: his hair is longish and cut at angles along his cheek bones, and his blue coat is fussy and exquisitely fitted, and his white pants match his white shirt and his suede shoes are an identical blue to his coat and all of this conglomerates into a man who's less threatening to X Parke than some men she's met and more importantly than the man who *could* have lured her into this car with only the sleight of a couple names and the simple promise of stories. But X Parke's less relieved by the dog, which sits on the car's soft burgundy-swathed floor near Samuel's blue-sueded feet and regards X Parke with an expression that conjures to mind the word 'pique' and is far and away the largest dog X Parke's ever seen, a Great Dane perhaps or even something larger whose face through the window betrayed only an insinuation of its total mass. Seated on the car's floor the dog's head manages to approach the car's ceiling more aggressively than Samuel's, and its paws are as wide and long as Samuel's pointed shoes, and its white collar, which seems fashioned from the same material as Samuel's pants and shirt, could likely serve as a belt for X Parke in a pinch. "This is Cabbage," Samuel says, placing his hand on the dog's mucronate cranium. X Parke waves at the dog and then entwines her fingers in the way the Jessas hate—and looks down briefly to check if it really does appear that doing so makes it look like she has extra fingers, which it actually kind of does—"You look so much like your mother," Samuel's saying. "So much like your mother but yet somehow nothing at all like your father . . ." The car's entire interior being overlayed in burgundy velvet or some other satiny material reminds X Parke of something she cannot immediately recall. And a stringent floral odor that X Parke can taste as she breathes through her mouth. Behind Samuel's a burgundy overlayed partition where presumably beyond is the car's driver. And there's music coming softly from speakers she cannot locate, a violin and a cello, perhaps, each sculpting its own asynchronous melody.

"How far are we," X Parke asks, "from my family's home?"

"Not far," Samuel eyes X Parke's sweater. "Why do you dress so frumpily? Is it to dissuade the attention of oglers? You must be offput by all that attention, if you have anything remotely like your mother's body. Ugh, your mother's body. To use a colloquialism: it's insane."

Cabbage adjusts his haunches and chews his tongue around his mouth.

"The first time I laid my eyes on her—it feels like decades ago though it was only this past autumn—when she answered the door upon my arrival for our initial consultation in her workout clothes, glistening from her exercise . . . ohhh . . ." Samuel scootches himself nearer to Cabbage. "I was instantly moved. And I have not stopped moving since. In fact I am moving right now."

X Parke closes her eyes so she can roll them without Samuel's detection, then offers a petite and toothless smile and a shrug that she hopes conveys something like polite disinterest. This is not the first time X Parke's encountered lustfulness directed at her mom; X Parke remembers in high school accompanying her parents to the spring teacher conferences, going from classroom to classroom to speak with X Parke's various teachers—Ms. Inoue among them—and detecting from the other students and parents and even teachers an inordinate amount of uncontrolled fasciculations, though in reaction to what at first X Parke couldn't discern until toward the end of the day as she'd waited by the school's entrance while her parents chatted with another pair of parents down the hall and a group of boys in X Parke's grade approached and sidled and leaned up to X Parke all with the same face on their faces and one'd stood very near X Parke and said pretty loudly, "Your mom's a dime," and another'd added even more loudly, "I want to hide stuff in her," and they'd all cackled and X Parke'd told them to engage in some form or another of self-fornication and removed herself to the immediate outside of the school building and sulked there until her parents emerged and on the way home in the backseat of her family's car she'd said "Some boys told me they want to hide stuff in you," and X Parke's mom had remained still facing the windshield and replied that "Boys will be boys," and X Parke's dad'd reached over from the driver's seat and placed his wide, lined hand on the inside of her mom's upper thigh and they'd driven on. And then of course there was the one time not long after that that she'd invited her friend, the non-boyfriend whose name she *still* can't remember, over to her house after school and spent most of the afternoon basically recreating their school-time sessions though in this case they sat on the floor outside X Parke's dad's office and listened to music and at one point the boy'd excused himself to use the bathroom and disappeared down the hall and after ten or so minutes X Parke'd grown uneasy at his continued absence and so went to check on him and found the bathroom empty and continued on along the hall checking each room until she'd made it to her parents' bedroom on the far side of the house and peeked in, genuinely expecting it to be empty, and found her non-boyfriend supine on her parents' bed with his pants unfastened and his knifish penis in his hand and a pair of X Parke's mom's underwear bunched into his mouth, and X Parke'd sort of froze and watched this revolting scene for a few seconds longer than she should've before backing slowly away and returning to the floor outside her dad's office and listening to music on her own until the non-boyfriend returned five or so minutes later and apologized for getting lost on his way to and from the bathroom and sat next to X Parke and reinserted his headphone and the two had worn on the afternoon thus until the non-boyfriend's ride showed up and he'd gone home and X Parke never mentioned that she'd seen him and certainly never mentioned anything to her mom or dad about it and thought about it a lot after it happened but then less and less as time went on and in fact hadn't really thought about it at all in maybe a year until now.

Meanwhile Samuel Grillet's going on from his seat opposite X Parke's and tracing furrows into Cabbage's humungous head. ". . . I've never met a woman like Reinemarie—and I've met a few women, as one does in my line of work. But never one like her, as alluring and electric and communicative. She's become the mantle of my heart's palace, the hands of my longing arms. We barely speak—we hardly need to—other than about the market, about stocks and bonds, and yet laced within this business are all the tacit signals, the sidelongs and normal rates of breathing that are more than enough to know that I love her. I am in love with her, with your mother, X Parke. And she is in love with me. And today is the day we tell your father we are in love."

X Parke counts her fingers from her sight's lower periphery. "You and my mom have plans to tell my dad you're in love?"

"Yes!" Samuel's hand flutters over Cabbage's head, then lands. "Well, yes, though we have not discussed it outright. As I said, she and I manage to communicate through gesture and distance, to weave intricate dialogues even when we are not in the same room. We have agreed without speaking that today is the day we break your father's heart. There is no good time for this. And no better time than now."

"I see."

"We have written to each other, your mother and I. Well, I have written to her. She does not need to respond because I already know everything she would say. And technically I have never delivered any of my letters to her, but again, she receives them merely by existing on the same ravaged earth as I." Samuel probes the inside of his coat with an unguis of lengthy fingers and produces a fold of yellow pages. "I keep the letters here. I would happily share them with you, though I fear they are . . . inappropriate for a little girl. Our love is explicit, Reinemarie's and mine. Well, implicitly explicit. We are not offput by the less wholesome fabrics of each other's bodies. Nothing is merely hers nor mine; our privacies are inclusive enough for us both. But I don't imagine a little girl—no matter how strikingly she inherits her mother's insane beauty—would appreciate any of this about which I speak."

Through the car's window the mountains are a wall clung with snowy forest, X Parke craning to see the peaks hidden above the window's top border but cannot crane enough without needing to effectively lie down in the backseat, chewing her lip at a gash in the mountain's face where a section of trees and silver rock are torn away and the ruddy dirt beneath is exposed and X Parke strains her sight toward the shadowy edge of the gash where just under the still-standing trees at its perimeter there's something gray scurrying and pausing at the exposed dirt's edge and then scurrying beneath the tree cover as the car goes on.

"My own mother," Samuel continuing, "was a different kind of woman. She was beautiful too, I suppose, early on. Another kind of beautiful. Pretty, I would say. And she was happy, I think, on the outside. She sang around the house, my mother, sang and trilled and whistled. Always music outpouring from her. This is indicative of happiness. My mother was happy and pretty. And I was her health proxy, which is relevant, because she collapsed, my mother, in her bathroom one afternoon in early spring. I remember it was a beautiful day. And I found her there when she did not appear for our usual coffee date in the atrium. I found her half in and half out of the shower, the water spattering like oil, her face distended on one side and her hands knotted strangely with some of the fingers erected and others curled down, and I did the only thing a son can do in such a scenario: I covered her with a towel, and then I called an ambulance. And at the hospital they told me she'd had a stroke, my mother, and been intubated, and so could not speak, and could neither sing nor whistle. Nor trill. I held her hand in intensive care, which was a fine hand—not remotely as shapely and sensual as *your* mother's hand, but delicate and *pretty*, in its own way—and I bobbed my head, I recall, to the metronomic beeping of the machines around her bed, not deliberately but just by instinct, as if in a trance. And the doctors told me they'd found a hole in my mother's heart, which would have caused the stroke, and that they recommended operating as immediately as possible, and I being my mother's health proxy, as I mentioned, was forced then and there to grant permission for this emergency heart operation about which I asked repeatedly from my mother's bedside was it necessary? And the doctors said something along the lines of 'Nothing is necessary,' which was very helpful, and ultimately I opted for the surgery, since had I not, and had she died from my inaction, then I would have had to live with this indecision, whereas if she died during or after the surgery then at least I could say I did something, anything, and could live with myself. And alas that is what happened, with my pretty mother going and dying on the operating table with her heart open to the dry light of the world from which the random forces of nature have long conspired to conceal it, she died there having never woken from the stroke, and I like to think her final memory was from back in the shower, applying one of her myriad face scrubs or exfoliators and excited for our daily coffee date. And I was not mad at myself nor did I harbor any guilt, for I had done my due diligence and the best I could for her, and besides she left behind a great deal of money and the family's company, the accounting firm for which I am now the sole partner—which I understand is somewhat counterintuitive—and with this company and with the substantial fortune I inherited I do my absolute best to honor and perpetuate my mother's good name, for her name was good in the financial advising and accounting industry, and to this day she is occasionally mentioned with reverence and come to think of it—and I should remember to include this in my next letter to your mother—were it not for my mother's untimely stroke and my decision to grant permission for the surgery that killed her then I never would have met *your* mother, since I expanded the jurisdiction of our firm upstate, a decision my mother, while alive, would have abhorred, and so ultimately my mother's death led me to Reinemarie, who is the love of my life and my reason for living and which pales every bliss and tragedy held aside it, and so I am guiltless in my mother's death and in fact I am glad that she's dead."

There's a lull now in the music and a burgundy silence with both Samuel and Cabbage eyeing X Parke as if she's got food on her face and she's compelled to fill the silence though the moment she speaks the music resumes. "And your dad?" she asks.

"Fathers don't matter," Samuel Grillet traces his mouth's outline with one hand and traces a facsimile of his mouth on Cabbage's head with the other. "They could be anyone."

X Parke nods slowly and moves her eyes as if to trail a zagging thought. "I'm not convinced my mom has ever told you a story about me. Or told you anything about anything other than her finances. Implicitly or otherwise."

Cabbage mewls as Samuel's fingernails rake his cranium, and the violin and cello—or though maybe now it's only one of them, or a third instrument entirely—slope and moan and chirp an augmented arpeggio, and Samuel Grillet's squinting at X Parke and his mouth's a taut line through the middle of his face. A raggy shape darts past the car's window in the opposite direction of the car, a bird or a leaf, and X Parke smoothes the satiny seat. "You're a wayward little girl," Samuel's lips quaver inside a narrow ambit. "Your mother's told me *everything*. She's told me what she's afraid of and what she isn't afraid of. She's told me her divinest truths and her dirtiest fantasies. She's told me your father is a brute and a dullard and has not stimulated her physically or emotionally or mentally *ever. Ever.* She's told me her life is a husk of the one she envisioned, that she regrets every choice she's made until she met me and chose to love me. She told me she regrets shackling herself to a dull man and hates herself for bearing his dull children. She told me that having children ruined her, that when *you* came out you came out feet-first and hurt her so bad that part of her now trails behind and outside of her and can never come home. You evicted your mother's spirit."

"I did not."

"Yes you did. You evicted her spirit and then you stomped on her spirit until it was in pieces and you complained that she'd gotten her spirit on your shoes. You refused her ceaseless love and her careful consideration, she told me. She told me you're a wayward little bitch who came out feet-first and broke her spirit with your needy little mind and that's why your father left us."

X Parke frowns.

"Er . . ." Samuel paws nervously at Cabbage. "I mean . . . never mind that last thing. But everything else is true. As true as your mother's love for me."

"So entirely in your head then."

"Despicable little tramp. You inherited none of your mother's grace."

X Parke presenting Samuel with the side of her face and looking out through the car's window where the forest has thickened around the car and white vertices whip past and X Parke wonders whether they're on a road or just driving along the forest's raw ground. Cabbage now yawning mightily and stooping so his tremendous head dangles near the car's burgundy upholstered floor and he sniffs at something there nonchalantly with his eyes craned up toward X Parke, Samuel having replaced the fold of yellow papers back into his coat and shaking his head so his hair bobbles against his cheekbones and one hand drums its fingers tersely along his thigh. X Parke feeling graceless and irked and but shrugging and forgoing grace for graciousness by saying, "Thanks for the ride, though," to which Samuel huffs and uncrosses and then recrosses his legs and folds his arms across his chest in such a way that X Parke's made to feel as if she's been unfair or reactionary without considering the entire situation or else missing some central aspect of the situation entirely and being reminded of the weirdest thing about how her relationship or non-relationship with her high school non-boyfriend ended or didn't end, whereby in the spring soon after she'd caught him in her parents' bedroom—which she never disclosed to him—he began acting in such a way toward X Parke that she was made to feel as if she'd done something wrong, for example just the next week in school while she was sitting in their usual spot by the handicap bathroom during a free period with one earphone lodged in her ear and the other dangling free in her lap, she'd seen him approaching from the main hallway and he'd kind of smirked at her and then pivoted and headed off in another direction, and then later she'd seen him again only this time he was with another girl, a pretty girl in a red satiny coat who X Parke'd never seen, and the two had come down the hall and glanced over their shoulders toward X Parke and the non-boyfriend had said something from the side of his mouth and the girl had laughed and leaned against him and the two had walked off together and X Parke had set her hands on her knees and breathed normally. And this was just the start of it because a day or two after that X Parke'd come into school and seen him, the non-boyfriend, standing by some lockers with some other boys and she'd approached and said, "Hey" and the non-boyfriend had looked at her and looked her up and down and snickered and said, "Uh, hey," and the other boys had also snickered and X Parke'd asked, "Are we hanging today?" and the non-boyfriend'd looked at the other boys with this crooked smile and they'd smiled crookedly back at him and he'd said, "Naw," in this drolling sort of affected way and the other boys had laughed and one had said something that sounded like, "Not enough hand," and then they'd all walked off and left X Parke standing there feeling very cold. And later that same week or the week after, X Parke'd been on her way to Ms. Inoue's Philosophy of Science elective and'd been passing through the library to get there and was running a little early but wanted to try to catch Ms. Inoue before class to ask her for some clarification on the reading, which was an excerpt from Hume's *An Enquiry Concerning Human Understanding* that X Parke'd had a hard time with specifically as it pertained to Hume's insistence on some 'universal principle' guiding a sequence of thoughts through their iterations, since X Parke could neither find in the text nor imagine on her own an example of what this principle might be and was afraid she was missing or misunderstanding something, and as she'd been navigating the library's stacks—which were arranged in such a way that she needed to zigzag through a superfluity of passages in order to arrive at the conference room at the library's back—she'd heard a gasp from nearby and paused to look up and down the passages, where she didn't immediately see anyone or anything, and so had continued on with the spines of the books like branchless trees and then heard the sound again nearer and discerned it was coming from the stacks' passage parallel to hers and'd pressed an ear against the books there to listen and the gasp had come again and there was another sound, two voices—one male one female—coaxing or chanting the same words over and over and X Parke'd very carefully slid a book from the shelf and peered through the slit which was wide enough to espy a rectangle of the parallel passage where the non-boyfriend was stooped forward on his knees on the floor's shorn carpet rummaging his hands inside a flank of pale skin and bunched green felt with his lips puckered and his eyes taut, the gasping coming from out of frame in front of the non-boyfriend and X Parke's eyes spiraling for more information, the chanting also from out of frame behind the non-boyfriend and the non-boyfriend rummaging harder and sweating and then drawing back his hands cupped as if with water and quavering and X Parke's eye straining to see and seeing in the cupped hands a small raggy object which bristled and unfurled a tiny head with a translucent beak and pared black eyes, the non-boyfriend turning now carefully with his cupped hands outstretched and presenting them behind him where another pair of hands, these mantled in ink, received the small raggy creature and bundled it quickly in a swatch of red cloth and withdrew it from frame and a deep voice lauded, "We're proud of this one," and the non-boyfriend turned back to the flank of skin and bunch of green felt and meekly rolled a pair of stockings up along the flank and then rolled down the green felt over the stockings and X Parke'd set the book she'd taken off the shelf on the floor's shorn carpet and retreated back through the maze of stacks and out of the library and ended up skipping Philosophy of Science that day and that afternoon outside the school she'd seen the non-boyfriend sitting on the low wall surrounding the flagpole with one earphone in his ear and the other earphone in the ear of the pretty girl in the red satiny coat who looked older than him and X Parke and X Parke'd walked right past and headed home and'd taken a shortcut across the tracts of feral meadows at the town's outskirts where her passage startled a thousand birds nesting in the sharp grass so they took all to the sky at once and screamed and whorled around her like brains of smoke.

The car now slowing and turning and trundling through a ditch, Samuel Grillet eyeing X Parke from across the car and sitting in such a way that X Parke feels he's very close though he's at the same distance he's been this whole time. Cabbage smelling around the car's burgundy floor with his eyes lifted also at X Parke and X Parke looking at the space somewhere between the dog and the man as if either may start to speak at any moment. The car slows further and turns again and its tires crunch gravel at a steep incline, X Parke glancing out the car's window where the stalks of white trees file sluggishly as if depressed or very sleepy and X Parke yawns and Cabbage yawns and Samuel Grillet covers his mouth with a fan of slender and manicured fingers and his eyes crease. The trees now give way abruptly onto a long lawn sloping upward and speckled with birch copses and at its crest an enormous and stately mansion replete with stone columns and pillars of white smoke lazing from the stoic chimneys and countless pupil-less windows unblinking from its many stories. X Parke turning to the car's opposite window where the lawn slopes down toward a glassy pond hemmed on three sides with snowless greenery and beyond that a low and ordered woods and beyond the woods a distant white valley smoldering with young sunlight and low frothy clouds.

"Where are we?" X Parke asking, all her fingers entwined.

"Your home, girl," Samuel strokes Cabbage's haunch. "You're home."

"This is not my home."

"Of course it is," Samuel's bangs dangle. "Though . . . it occurs to me now that of course you would not yet have seen the new additions. See, since I've been employed by your parents to account for their finances their wealth has expanded somewhat generously. I have this effect on people. And your mother of course deserves so much better than your father could provide. She deserves wealth commensurate with her insane beauty. This is where I stepped in. The new house and the property is just part of it. There are also stocks and bonds and other invisible assets. You will be happy with the new conditions. Anyone would."

The car zigzags toward the mansion. "What happened to the old house? To *my* house?"

"I don't know why you care. But it remains at the edge of the property. All your parents did, at my recommendation, was purchase the adjacent land to build on. Land value, as you likely don't know, can only ever increase. Your parents have made an intelligent investment in their futures and in yours. As for the old house, I suggested they repurpose it as a shed, though I believe they have other plans."

"What other plans?"

Samuel Grillet tents his fingers and closes his eyes. "Ask them. I am tired of explaining every little inconsequential thing to you."

The car now veering right alongside a row of tall hedges that flank the window and obscure the mansion from X Parke, and X Parke feels this very familiar but yet unplaceable sadness or panic or maybe guilt burble and knurl in her tummy and she further entwines her fingers which for a frightening moment seems about all she really can do at all to combat or offset the sad panic guilt and which is frightening because it is nothing but a vapid gesture as useless as waving in an empty room and the sad panic guilt—which is frightening on a distended level from the inherent fright within the sad panic guilt because she doesn't understand what's causing it or why it's so distantly familiar—threatens to climb through her like ivy or a virus and sicken or suffocate her until now she remembers, as the car churns to a stop and the music cuts out and the sound of the driver's door opening and footsteps on gravel and the backseat door opens and Cabbage lopes out with Samuel in tow and acrid sunlight bubbles into the car and makes the burgundy upholstery look orange as if it's been orange this whole time, something Malory'd said in the dark, that nothing is real, that their lives are metaphors for something else and everything that happens to them is an allusion to a realer thing that itself alludes to an even realer thing and so on. And X Parke feels instantly and veritably relieved and follows Samuel from the car's backseat and Cabbage leads them along the hedge and through a gap in the hedge to a narrow set of mossy steps that maunder upward through further hedge and natty leafless branches to a green flaking door that is also so familiar and yet unplaceable beneath a rocky eave from which dangle a set of lifeless wind chimes and Samuel opens the door and Cabbage disappears through it and X Parke flinches as if she expects birds or bats or something to fly from the doorway and braid themselves into her hair and cork themselves into the holes in her face and make of her body a convenience, a wandering home.

12

The mansion's immediate interior is smelling a lot like tobacco smoke to X Parke which's confusing as neither of her parents are smokers or at least she doesn't think they are. Here's a narrow mudroom with a low bench along one wall and a collection of unfamiliar shoes lined beneath the bench, on the opposite wall a hand-sized painting of either an obscured face or a tapered landscape inside an ornate brass frame twice as thick on each side as the painting itself. The floor is concrete or something and the walls are plaster. X Parke removes her Converse and sets them beneath the bench with the other shoes, then discovers that Cabbage and Samuel Grillet haven't waited for her and have disappeared and she's alone. Somewhere off in the mansion's bowels or reaches: voices. The smell of tobacco smoke's aggressive. Immediately beyond the mudroom's a larger wood-paneled room with doorways set at incongruous points on each wall and a circular rug in its middle with what look like concentric red circles though as X Parke looks closer is actually a tightly coiled spiral. From the doorway to her right a guttering glow, X Parke now going this way and peering around the door's frame before passing into a room with no furniture or windows and an enormous stone mantle at the far end in which a well-tended fire crepitates, X Parke sort of pausing at the room's threshold and crossing her arms from a sudden chill or anticipation of chill and calling: "Hello?" in a way such that her voice sounds different than it usually does to her, the way your own voice sounds when you hear it played back on a recording and wonder who you really are. The ceiling in this room is low whereas X Parke suspects she could brush it with her fingertips were she to jump though she refrains and paces along the room's perimeter where many more doorways gape onto darkness and calls again, "Hello?" and allows a bank of hair to rampart half her face until she's overwhelmed by the anxiety that whatever section of the room is obscured by her bank of hair is containing something that lurks or looms beside her and breathes on her and will remain there as long as she can't see it and quickly bunches the hair back behind her ear and sees nothing in the retrieved section of room except the fire's light guttering along the walls and the many hands and teeth of hot light of it.

"Hello," X Parke says now as if to someone here, and is promptly shushed from one of the doorways. "Shhh," says a voice from the dark doorway, "Everyone'll hear us." X Parke straining to see and seeing the voice attached to a small body there, glasses refracting the mantle's chatter, and the voice familiar enough: the voice of X Parke's sister, Hobbes Nicole, eleven or twelve now X Parke cannot remember, skulking up and down just inside the darkened mouth of the doorway.

"Who will hear us?" X Parke's saying, standing just outside the doorway with the fireplace and its heat on her back.

Hobbes Nicole kneading something in her stout fingers and seeming—though X Parke cannot tell for certain given the fire refracting in her glasses and obscuring her eyes—to be looking at the floor beside X Parke rather than at X Parke herself.

"Everyone," Hobbes Nicole stage whispers. "They told me I had to go to my room but I came down here instead and if they find me they'll make me go to my room and I *hate* it up there."

Footsteps whine along the ceiling. "What's so wrong with your room?"

"It's too big and when I'm alone in it there's this thing that hides at the foot of my bed or if I go and look at the foot of my bed then it moves to the other side of my bed or if I look there it moves again and I don't think it's mean or anything but it doesn't want me to see it which makes me think it's trying to hide something from me or that maybe it actually *is* mean but if it was mean and wanted to hurt me then it would have done it by now because it's had plenty of opportunity to hurt me while I'm sleeping or even while I'm awake and alone in my room and but it hasn't yet and so I don't think it wants to hurt me just hide something from me, which I don't like. Anyway what are you doing here?"

X Parke's nose is runny a little and she sniffles and wipes at her upper lip with a bare forearm. "I'm on winter break."

"But why'd you come in with Mr. Grillet?"

"He gave me a ride. I was walking and he recognized me I guess from some pictures in the house and he gave me a ride. Do you like him?"

"He stares at mom a lot. But his dog's nice and doesn't have awful breath like most dogs. His dog's breath's better than most humans' breath actually. Did you know that dogs only use one lung at a time when they breathe? Like they alternate lungs?"

"That doesn't sound right."

"Why were you walking? Why didn't you take a taxi?"

"I don't know. Oh, because my plane crashed, can you believe that? It crashed somewhere halfway between college and here and I had to walk through the woods for days. I don't know how many days exactly, more than two."

"Your plane crashed, X Parke?"

"Yes. Actually."

"Was everyone alright?"

"I don't know. I was. The woman who sat next to me was alright, I think. I saw her after . . . She had these awful tennis ball green fingernails."

"Tennis balls are yellow."

"Whatever."

"Well mom and dad didn't know you were coming because if they did they would have told me because I'm always asking about when you're coming back and they always say 'I don't know' which I can tell is true because they don't do it in the way where their voice goes up and their eyebrows go up like when they're lying but rather just in the normal way where they say it without stopping what they're doing which means they're telling the truth because lying is complicated and people can't usually lie while also doing something else at the same time so anyway they didn't know you were coming because they would have told me because I ask them when you're coming all the time because I miss you."

"I miss you too, Hobbes."

"Hobbes Nicole."

"Hobbes Nicole. How's school?"

"School's alright I like history."

"What are you learning about?"

"The Fire and the bad stuff before the Fire. It's really interesting because it's like Mrs. Grenier said that there's before the Fire and there's after the Fire and everything before the Fire was one way and everything after the Fire is another way and that it's interesting and important because there's nothing else really like that in all of human history except sometimes I don't know if that's true because when we see pictures from before and read things about it it doesn't seem that different from now at all except for a few little things which are negligible."

"That's a great word."

"Negligible is a great word."

"Hobbes Nicole I have a question."

"You don't need to say you have a question you can just ask the question because saying you have a question before asking a question is redundant and being redundant makes people look like they're hiding something."

"Do you remember when you were little? Like really little?"

"Uh huh."

"Like when you were four or five. Or six."

"Uh huh."

"What do you remember?"

"You mean in general?"

"No, I mean, I guess I mean do you remember *me* at all from when you were that little? Any specific memories about me?"

"Uh huh."

"Like what?"

"Well I remember playing hide and seek with the Quay family every spring in their gardens don't you?"

"Yeah. Remind me."

"Well we only ever played in the spring because in the winter it was too cold and then they all left every summer I don't know where they went but in the spring the grass was so green and lush and there were Easter-egg colored birds zagging through the grass and robins in the trees and the Quay family had those sprawling gardens remember with the big stone sculptures that weren't really shaped like anything in particular maybe really big people kind of but mostly nothing and Pembroke who you know he was the oldest Quay brother he would always play the seeker because he was too fat to hide remember and so he would sit on top of the tallest sculpture in the middle of the garden surrounded by all the smaller sculptures and the pink and bright green trees with the robins in them and it was always a beautiful day with a rich blue sky and fluffy white clouds drifting along but never in front of the sun and it was always just a little chilly but not too chilly to be outside and we as in me and all the other Quay children would hide in the gardens usually behind the sculptures or else just face-down in the grass sometimes if we though it would conceal us from Pembroke who would close his eyes and count to a hundred or sometimes fifty but usually a hundred though sometimes he would count really fast so it was more like fifty even if he said all the numbers from one to a hundred it was still more actually like fifty and then he would open his eyes and he had these really beady silver eyes that I always thought looked like coins which I always thought was appropriate because the Quays had a lot of money and so it made sense that their eyes or other parts of their bodies would look like money like with Treva Quay whose skin was the same color as pennies and anyway Pembroke would open his coiny eyes and then without leaving his perch on the tall middle sculpture he would peer around the gardens and kind of swivel his really wide bottom on the sculpture and peer and try to catch glimpses of people behind the other sculptures or sneakily facedown in the grass and no matter how well anyone thought they'd hid he'd always see them and call them out by name and make them come out from their hiding spots and go stand in a circle around the base of his sculpture facing out and I always used to wonder how he got up onto the sculpture because he really was pretty fat though I know you aren't supposed to call people fat it's just that he was and it's not a bad thing about him it's just the case and but anyway I used to love to hide in this one spot that wasn't entirely behind a sculpture but was kind of just to the side and I would press myself down into the grass really deep so the dirt would sort of hug my body and the colorful birds zagging through the grass would have to zag around me and I discovered pretty early on that the only way to avoid Pembroke seeing you since his coiny eyes were so good at seeing things was to not stay still for long like for example after he would finish counting down from a hundred or fifty you would stay still and hope he didn't see you first, and when he called on someone else for them to come out and stand at the base of his sculpture you would kind of gauge the sound of his voice to know what direction he was facing in since you really couldn't see him because your face was pressed into the dirt like I said and if he did sound to be facing away from you you would then crawl maybe five or ten feet through the grass and then stop and let him peer and scan and whatever until he called someone else and then you would crawl some more and then stop again and for whatever reason this really worked really well to keep him from seeing you because Pembroke was kind of like a toad in that way meaning like did you know that toads can only see things that they've looked at twice or more than twice but everything they only look at once they can't see and I know I know you're gonna say that isn't true or it doesn't sound true but it is and anyway the only time I ever won at hide and seek with the Quay family was by using this crawl-stop strategy and it was exciting because I don't think the Quays were used to not at least one of them winning whatever they were doing and so it felt extra good to know I'd taught them something about what it's like to not win which Mrs. Grenier says is the most important thing to learn like she even said once that you could forget everything you ever learned about when you won or did something right and only remember the times you lost or did something wrong and you would be better for it and the world would be a better place for it so I remember that from when I was five and six and seven I think until the Quays left one summer to go wherever they went and they never came back."

"Where am I in that story?"

"Oh I guess I don't actually remember if you were there or not but I remember being facedown in the grass really well and the smell of the dirt and the Easter-egg colored birds zagging through the grass and sometimes through my hair and I even remember once an earthworm came out of the ground while I was being still and Pembroke I think was looking right at me but hadn't noticed me yet and the worm wriggled against my eye and poked around in my nostril and I couldn't move because then he would have seen me and I would have lost and did you know earthworms are the only animal besides humans that use verbs to communicate?"

"Do you have any memories about *me*, Hobbes Nicole?"

"Yeah but I can't think of any. Oh, I remember when we all went rafting on the Wallkill River you me and mom and dad one summer with that guy whose name I can't remember but he was the guide or the captain or whatever people in charge of rafts are called and we were all five of us on the raft going down the river in the river's middle and it was a calm part of the river meaning there weren't any rapids or anything like there'd been downstream but just glassy water all drifting along with the rock walls on either side remember like a canyon and I kept calling it a canyon but the guide or captain kept correcting me and saying it was called something else I can't remember what but I do remember there was an eagle or a hawk circling this section of the rock wall way high up that jutted up like a spire and it kept glinting in the sun when it circled at a certain point so it looked like it was on fire and anyway I looked over at you because you were there sitting next to me and at one point when I looked over at you you were crying or tears were coming out of your eyes and you were sad but we were in the back of the raft and mom and dad and the guide or captain were all busy looking ahead at the river and the canyon or whatever it was called and they didn't notice you were crying and you weren't making any noise or anything just crying silently in the raft and I didn't know what you were crying about and you didn't tell me but I remember I started to cry too because . . . well I don't know why I guess just because you were crying and if you were crying then there must have been something wrong and something to cry about and so I started crying and you and I were crying silently together in the back of the raft drifting down the middle of the Wallkill River while the eagle or hawk or whatever was circling in the sun and then you looked over and saw I was crying too and as soon as you saw I was crying you stopped crying and asked what was wrong and I didn't know what was wrong so I think I shrugged or shook my head and you put your arm around me and but I didn't feel sad anymore because you weren't sad anymore and so I stopped crying right away and I thought to myself that maybe you would have thought that you made me stop crying because you put your arm around me and that you made me feel better about whatever I was sad about but that's not really what happened because I wasn't sad about anything except you being sad and when you weren't sad anymore I wasn't sad either."

"I don't remember that."

"I remember it really well I think about it all the time."

"I don't even remember going rafting."

"It was alright I don't like getting wet and it's almost impossible not to get wet on a raft but the river was really beautiful and the guide or captain whose name I can't remember knew a lot about the river like for example he told us there were over fifteen thousand different species of fish living in the river and even a species of dolphin though the dolphins only went to the river in the winter to breed and then swam back to the ocean for the rest of the year but in the winter sometimes they would come out through holes in the ice on the river's shallow edges and lay on the ice and sun themselves and sing this song that the guide or captain imitated and which sounded like *oooooeh-oooooeh* like that and they would do it all together at the same time and he said in the winter if you hear them from far away it sounds like people chanting."

"So mom and dad are upstairs?"

"They're in the viewing room with everyone but I'm going to stay down here because I don't want them to see me and if you see them you can't tell them you saw me because they'll make me go to my room and I hate it there because it's too big and there's this thing that hides at the foot of my—"

"I know, you told me."

"Yeah and so anyways they're upstairs in the viewing room."

"I don't know where that is."

Hobbes Nicole weaves in the shadowy mouth of the doorway and her glasses flare and she has something in her hands. "I'll show you I guess but we have to be quiet and I won't go all the way there with you okay?"

"Okay."

"Okay." Hobbes Nicole now turning and vanishing into the dark and X Parke following, the fire's meager light quickly evaporating and X Parke needing to grope out for a wall for guidance and foundering on her own feet when the hallway angles abruptly left and so then groping out for an indication of it and not finding the wall again and sort of splaying there in the dark and yelling, "Wait!"

"Shhh!" from directly in front of her. "Everyone'll hear us."

A clammy hand attaches to X Parke's and tugs her through the dark and X Parke's led onward this way and that and feeling with her free hand for a wall but there's no wall as she practices shaping the T word with her lips and rehearsing the cadence of her questions for her parents with her breath and imagining their faces softening next to one another's with mom on the left and dad on the right and here's a faint blue light now sculpting shapes ahead in the otherwise dark, and X Parke, who's started yawning and whose eyelids are leaden and whose feet feel each like fifty-pound weights fastened to the end of her legs, attempts to energize or reinvigorate herself by categorizing her meager field of sight into WHAT I CAN SEE (BLUE) and WHAT I CANNOT (DARKNESS) and finds for the first category a hazy pall like smoke from beneath a doorway and then translucent slats like smoky twilight through narrow blinds and the outlines of rows of maybe vases or urns about X Parke's height on either side of her and now also the stray wiry hairs atop Hobbes Nicole's head wavering near X Parke's chest and backlit in blue light like the ramous and reaching branches of a distant tree and for the second category X Parke finds everything else. Hobbes Nicole's hand and X Parke's hand are not holding one another's exactly but are rather simply touching—or not touching depending on whether things can touch at all—palm-to-palm with Hobbes Nicole's palm guiding X Parke's as if scoring routes from a spout of water. There's this idea to which Prof Mel Lane had introduced X Parke about how successful storytelling avoids making assumptions about the world by merely cataloging objects. Lane said this is to dare the world to exist at all—since the world's existence is itself in perpetual question. X Parke goes back over the first (BLUE) column to account for the seeable parts of the unseen world, which if she understands Prof Lane's idea are assertions of proof that something or anything must exist or even can, though she suspects, as Hobbes Nicole now pauses and draws aside either a door or a curtain so that blue light puffs like steam and now guides X Parke onward, that just because she can see and name parts does not mean they are any more real then anything she cannot see or name.

Soon the blue light reddens and brightens and the Penate sisters arrive in a small hot room with a cast iron furnace burning a dense and low flame and at the room's end's a doorway through which a staircase buckles up and immediately turns out of sight. "These stairs lead to the first floor and the viewing room is just straight ahead and you can't get lost because it's light up there on account of all the windows but I'm not going any further now so I'll see you later and please don't leave without saying goodbye to me again." Hobbes Nicole paces along the room's wall fidgeting with something which's made of either paper or metal but of which X Parke still cannot make sense or identify. Tired as she is—she walked after all the whole previous night and the night before slept fitfully on a floor and the night before that stood awake before a burning fuselage in an icy forest and the night before *that*—she has this sleepy thought that since she can't identify the thing Hobbes Nicole's holding then it's like the thing isn't even really there . . . though of course she then revises this very, very sleepy thought toward rationalism which would determine that because she can see the thing and presumably touch it or smell it should it have a smell or even hear it if it makes any sound or were she to drop it on the floor then of course it exists whether it has a name or not. The initial thought was very sleepy indeed and rooted in some stony metaphysical whim for which X Parke has neither the patience nor the time, especially now as she pats Hobbes Nicole's shoulder and starts up the staircase to confront her parents about her memory problem and possible T and which she anticipates will play out any number of ways: they may assure her that she does of course have memories of her life before twelve or thirteen and prod this memory free with gentle reminders of her life then or present her with a childhood toy that opens the floodgates of her blocked memory and through which the first two thirds of her life will surge; or they may nod stoically and share a look between themselves and then explain to X Parke that they are aware of her memory problem and that there's a good reason for it, a very good reason, namely a T that she suffered around the age when the memory stopped, or a T that she suffered for many years leading up to the age when the memory stopped, and that this T has been known to them forever and but they didn't know how to broach it with her or decided not to broach it with her until she was older, which apparently she is now, and they may then take the time to explain to her in surgical detail the parameters of the T and all the mortifying ways it occurred and how the occurrence of this T manifested the two parts of X Parke's life, and maybe one of them would fetch a piece of paper or poster board and draw two columns and mark one PRE-T and the other POST-T and then categorize X Parke's life into each column carefully without skimping on any details; or the premise may catch her parents unaware whereas their eyes will get square and they'll kneel before her and pet her hair and say "Our little girl. Our little girl," and her dad will chew his top lip to keep from crying while her mom cries openly and they grieve their parental blind spots and pray they'd known and could have done something to protect her but it's too late now and she'll forever carry this T-tization and the curtains it drew over her early life and how could they not have seen it since now it's so clear; or X Parke will emerge from the top of the stairs and pass through room after magnificent room replete with florid furniture and sweeping views through expansive windows of sprawling gardens and the valley on one side and the intrepid silver mountains on the other and voices up ahead, in the "viewing room" as Hobbes Nicole called it, and X Parke will stand in the doorway of the viewing room with its ceiling painted like the underside of a frozen canopy and a circular table at its center conspicuously chairless and on its far side a window running the entire length of the wall where people are gathered with their backs to X Parke, speaking measuredly about something outside the window and X Parke recognizes Samuel Grillet's blue coat and precise haircut and there's Cabbage seated beside him with his head almost as high as Samuel's shoulder, and beside Samuel there're the backs of X Parke's mom and dad, her mom's hair braided down her spine in a way that's not typical and her dad's hair shorter and grayer than X Parke remembers and beside her dad's this boy's back she doesn't recognize in all black and shortish—shorter than her dad and with wild black hair—and to this boy's left's another man, a tall man with a white ponytail whose hand—steeped in confusing tattoos—pets spirals onto the back of the boy in black and X Parke has this moment where she feels like everything's out of alignment or else too aligned and to the ponytailed man's left there's a woman with short-cropped coral hair and swooping hips in a red dress and all six of them—seven including Cabbage—with their backs to X Parke and the wall-length window through which they all face revealing the downward sloping lawn and the lake or pond at its nadir framed with snowless greenery and which X Parke, taking little steps first to the long table, then around the long table toward the window, recognizes all at once as the same pond or lake she grew up beside, the one with her house on its northern bank, and as she recognizes the pond or lake she notices the house there, her house, just barely obscured behind the flora and exactly as she remembers it, the pine-colored front porch and the yellow door and the dented satellite dish poised off the eave, all the windows now dark and drawn and the whole house seeming to curl in on itself as if embarrassed, and X Parke remembers leaving the house to go to college, only moths ago though it feels like a lifetime, leaving the house and her parents on the porch waving and Hobbes Nicole still asleep upstairs, or not actually waving but rather just standing there and they may as well have been waving as X Parke actually herself waved from the backseat of the taxi that would take her to the airport and she stands now with her fingers entwined about fifteen paces back from the row of people at the window of this magnificent room with the high and raftered ceilings and the sunlight refracting from the polished floor and magnifying and the ponytailed man pats the back of the boy in black and says something in a deep voice that sounds to X Parke like "It should just use a little," and then removes his hand from the back and steps away from the boy, and X Parke's dad does the same on the other side so the boy is standing now alone enough to raise his arms out on either side which is what he does, dramatically as if to rouse an orchestra, and as he does the man with the ponytail begins to chant in his sonorous voice—"*Cashawn sul denoton, cashawn sul grammath*," —and the woman with the coral hair and red dress joins him, and Samuel Grillet joins him, and X Parke's toes curl as her parents, too, join him, and as they all chant, the boy in black with his arms raised up at forty-five-degree angles over his shoulders, through the window the house by the lake or pond seems to tremble, like through the haze over a hot road, and as X Parke watches, her many fingers knotted at her waist, she sees smoke, white smoke rising up from the house, from its seams and windows, and then a gasp of orange as if from deep in its bowels and so faint that X Parke thinks she imagined it until it comes again more violently and curdles and red flame belches through the circular attic window and laps at the house's eave, and another gasp of orange and red from one then the other second floor window, six voices intoning "*Cashawn sul mise*," and the pond or lake casting a pallid emulation of the fire at the sky, trees of white smoke combing up and braiding and the house's downstairs windows breaking and vomiting orange and red and blue fire, the fire carving the house's walls into open veins and X Parke untangling her fingers and reaching out for something to lean against but the table's too far behind her and there's nothing else and she teeters as her home—the home in which her earliest memory, the foot of her bed, resides—hemorrhages and screams with fire and she must have made a sound or some obtrusive gesture because the man with the ponytail turns now and grins at her with gold teeth and deep coulees around his colorless eyes like the bark of a dead oak, and the woman to his left with the pixie cut coral hair turns too and X Parke recognizes her virescent eyes from an art gallery near the college, the woman now jerking her head minutely as if signaling a line from X Parke to the burning house and something's hanging around her neck which she secures over her face, a pane of brindled fur tapered to a point around her nose and with two black beads for eyes, mouthless, and behind her through the window the old house is a wound of fire and X Parke's parents and Samuel Grillet and the woman behind her mask and the man with the ponytail—still grinning over his shoulder at X Parke—and even briefly X Parke thinks Cabbage the dog are all chanting "*Cashawn sul proxemicon, cashawn sul morand*," though of course the dog's not chanting but rather just chewing his enormous tongue around the inside of his mouth, X Parke upturning her hands and nodding at the man with the ponytail as if by way of protecting herself from him through a gesture of solidarity, and the man grins wider and his eyes flash past X Parke who turns to blink at the empty expanse from which I watch, and of course she sees nothing, and the man pats the boy in black on his back and the boy turns slowly toward X Parke and reveals a set of astounding blue eyes—not just the irises but the entire eyes—and the seething black spiral on his throat swirls inward to a point and X Parke's overcome by an impulse to rush either toward him or away from him and thus is struck motionless in her panicked ambivalence and Samuel Grillet turns now toward her too and scowls and places his hand on her mom's unmoving wrist and Cabbage yawns at her so now everyone except her parents is facing her and everyone except Malory is chanting, the words ballooning from their mouths and flattening and dissolving against the window's glass, and the house burns through the window as the woman with the mask ascends as if falling upward, her red dress flapping her onto a rafter overhead where she perches and tilts her pupil-less eyes glinting with the sun or the old house's fire down at X Parke and there's the tremor of bells as a shower of wires unfurl and skim the floor nearby and her parents' backs are so static that X Parke's gripped by this grotesque conviction that were they to turn there would be only more backs, and she folds her arms over her chest and shuts her eyes and abruptly the chanting stops.

Whereupon now reopening them the scene is unchanged—except for that the house by the pond or lake is indiscernible inside its castle of fire—X Parke emits a single tearless sob and squats on the floor and musses her hair across her face. Samuel Grillet now escorting her mom by the wrist away from the window to a doorway at the room's side and disappearing, Cabbage lumbering after and casting what X Parke reads or wants to read as an expression of sympathy over his tuberous shoulders. Her dad's still at the window with his hands at his sides and his hair gray and X Parke wants to see his face so bad that she calls to him but he remains still and the man with the ponytail, the Dean, winks at me. "Give it to us."

X Parke scoffs and her eyes search. Malory's expressionless blue eyes are fixed on her.

The Dean's eyes crease. "You've neither the permission nor the means to refuse us. We are asking you merely as a courtesy."

"I don't know what you want me to do," X Parke groans.

"Need we remind you of the alternative should you shirk your obligation here?" the Dean extracts a gnarled wooden pipe from somewhere and tamps its bowl with his thumb. "Need we go over again the nightmare of unending disassembly? The wandering? The wordlessness? You are a man with much to say, we understand, Mister Blythe. Show yourself, and give it to us, and your faculties will be restored."

X Parke's hands ball and she beats at her thighs. "Who are you *talking* to? What is going *on*? Dad? *Dad?* Please turn around! Daddy! *Dad!!!*"

Here I allow X Parke to sleep, gently, so her head wilts forward and she crumples to the side and her hair fans over her face, and I show myself.

"Good, Mister Blythe," the Dean sets his pipe in his lips and gestures to Malory, who lifts a finger as sparks hop from the bowl and blue smoke runnels from the Dean's nostrils. "We know you are not stupid. Now give it to us. Now."

I lean over X Parke's little sleeping body, her limbs tangled, and she smells like the forest, and delicately I unfasten my wires from her wrists and ankles and from her throat, and gather them and furl them over my shoulder, and I step back from her. For a moment she seems to stir, though I know this to be impossible.

There's the crinkle of bells and the wires hanging from the rafters drift across the floor and poise over X Parke, their fringes curling and tightening around her wrists and ankles and lifting her limp body upright so it dangles there with its socked feet an inch over the floor, and she floats now toward the window and sways to a stop between Malory and the Dean with her head forward and her eyelids down. The Dean chews a sheet of smoke forward in his mouth and draws the outside of an old hand down X Parke's bare arm. "Are we sure this is it?" he says.

Malory's uncompromised expression remains thus. "Yes," he says, his voice like wind through dead wood.

"It is done," the Dean says, his words carving script through his smoke, now wedging his pipe into the corner of his mouth and tenting his hands fingertip to fingertip so the ramous tattoos align like circuitry, arching one finger through the crook of another and angling his palms so the circuitry shifts, the lines on one hand feeding the lines on the other and now shaking both hands free as if to cast off water and there's rustling and the smell of wet earth, and a bird darts from behind me and smashes its skull into the window and plops to the floor—a flower of red mars the glass like a handprint—and I feel myself click back into place, the tired weight of my old body, the bad knee, the rusty musk of my breathing—and more pertinently the tired weight of my own thoughts, my own *voice*—for the first time in five-and-a-half years. And I bluster forward just barely catching myself from toppling face first to the floor, and thirsty, parched, my mouth and throat and stomach: dust; and my eyes bleary and needing also to piss so bad that I feel my kidneys swelling against my spine. And I am sad, and relieved of course. And so tired.

"That is all, then," the Dean is saying. Behind him, through the window, the old house is now a pulsing heap of molten ash. "Go live whatever's left of your life, if you choose. Next time you decide you've had enough, rest assured we will not again stand in your way."

The backs of my teeth are chalky, and my tongue is thick. "Go . . ." I clench my jaw and suck angrily at my saliva ducts for any semblance of moisture. I feel urine start to leak out of me, and cannot stop it. "Go . . . fuck yourself."

The Dean grins and his shoulders heave as if with laughter, though there's no sound. Malory's craning to see X Parke's face beneath her oily black hair. X Parke's dad hasn't moved from the window.

"Take us to the city, boy," the Dean reaches around X Parke and pats Malory's shoulder. "It's time they see us." Malory pries his pupil-less eyes from X Parke's downturned face as if with great effort and holds the Dean in his undemonstrative and yet irritated gaze for full seconds during which time the Dean appears, to my amusement and consternation, to shirk a layer or two of his composure and to shift his stance nervously. Then Malory flits a hand palm-up as if to tap the underside of a sinking balloon, and there is smoke threading from beneath his feet, and from beneath the Dean's feet, and oozing around X Parke and up to the rafters, and now spits of flame too which grasp and bellow around them, and from within the fire the Dean winks at me and says, "Mister Grillet will be happy to call you a car." And the flames waver and ebb and there's nothing there except X Parke's dad at the long window betraying the lawn and the pond or lake and the birch copses and the corpse of the old house and the sparkling valley beyond.

My body's as sullen as I remember, stiff and brittle, my lungs two misshapen stones, my heart scrambling prey in the basin of my ribcage. My throat inflamed. My fingernails gnarled and yellow. I assume the mess of wiry beard still hangs off my face, but cannot be bothered to feel for it. The front of my pants are soaked with piss. When I walk, I find my left hip clicks at the joint. My ears ring. I join X Parke's dad at the window and rest my forehead briefly on the glass; when I remove it, there's an oval of oil there, and I brush at it futilely, merely smearing it. The odor of pipe tobacco lingers, and I pat my pockets for a cigarette to no avail. "You don't happen to smoke," I say to X Parke's dad, whose profile, despite Samuel Grillet's insistence, resembles X Parke's so acutely that I clench my teeth to keep my chin from quavering. "I'm, uh

. . . I'm sorry about the pee smell," I dust at my crotch. "I'm not usually walking around like this—though it's not as far off as I'd like it to be . . ." X Parke's dad is as still and silent as the window's glass. He is a thin and well-shaved man, and much smaller in real life than X Parke remembers him, and though I never had children I can imagine that his grief here and now is immense, and is what renders him paralyzed, and perhaps as much to show him solidarity as to comfort myself with human contact after these years of unimaginable distance, I place a hand on his shoulder, and his shoulder sinks inward, and his head lops sideways and his body cants and deflates and the whole thing crumples like an empty bag to the floor, where it is indiscernible from a hastily folded blanket or a pile of unwashed clothes.

I find Samuel Grillet and Reinemarie Penate in what must be the dining room, which is adjacent to the viewing room by a stubby hallway lined with electric candles. They are seated at opposite ends of a long table, dining from bowls of soup, not speaking. When I enter, Samuel Grillet sniffs the air, then turns to me and scowls. "Another mess he left for me," he says, clanking his spoon on the lip of his bowl and dabbing at his chin with a lacy handkerchief. "I suppose you're looking for some form of reparation for your quote unquote trouble. He told me this might happen. Very well, I have my checkbook, let's negotiate a reasonable sum." He slips a beak of fingers into his coat and removes a checkbook and pen. "You are a writer, yes? Not the most lucrative profession, but I understand you've had a deal of success. What was the advance on your last book, let's start there. I'll have to verify how often you publish, and take a look at sales, but I think we'll reach an agreeable sum for your lost time, plus a severance fee, of course . . ."

"Your daughter was extraordinarily astute," I say to Reinemarie, approaching the table.

She sips from her spoon, her eyelids lowered.

Samuel Grillet rises halfway and snaps his fingers in my direction. "You have nothing to say to her. You and I are discussing finances, and she's attempting to enjoy her lunch. Now if you'll be so kind . . ."

"The Dean told me no one ever realizes when they're . . . the way she was," I say. "But your daughter knew something was wrong. She didn't know how to make sense of it, but she knew . . . Sometimes it almost felt like she was having thoughts *with* me, or *for* me, like she knew I was there . . ."

"Cabbage!" Samuel Grillet strikes the table and the enormous dog lumbers from the corner of the room and positions himself between Reinemarie and myself. Speckles of foam cling to his jowls, and he seems to shake his head presagely.

"I don't want anything from you," I say first to Reinemarie, then turn and repeat to Samuel. "I don't want anything from either of you. I want to go home. And I want you to know that your daughter was extraordinary. And that she had questions for you that now she'll never have answered."

Reinemarie's spoon is halfway to her lips, and it stops there and her eyelids rise and the corner of her mouth curls minutely.

"My daughter always has many questions. She is upstairs in her room and will come down for lunch presently. Then she can ask me anything she wants, and I will answer her questions."

"No," I say, and I smell the fetid odor of my own breath. "Your other daughter. X Parke. The one you gave away."

Reinmarie slurps her soup and her lip curls higher. "What a silly name," she says.

"That's enough," Samuel Grillet flutters a hand. "If you don't want to be paid then you will leave now. My car will take you home. If you refuse, I will have Cabbage chew your brain out of your greasy head."

Reinemarie's eyes are as dead as beads.

I sigh. "Eighty thousand."

Samuel tsks and leans over his checkbook.

"That was the advance on my last novel. I typically produce a book every three to seven years, so for these last five and a half let's assume one book. My standard royalty these days is twelve point five percent for the first fifty thousand copies and fourteen percent for everything beyond, and given the length of my career and the ostensibly well-earned accolades, I can expect to sell around two hundred to five hundred thousand copies of a novel in its first year. I suspect most of these are being bought by colleges and universities, but no matter. I'll let you do the math on all that. And for damages just take whatever number you come up with and add a zero at the end."

Samuel Grillet blinks at me once, then scribbles out a check, tears it free, folds it in half and holds it in my direction between two protracted fingers like it's a bag of fresh dog shit. "Take it and leave," he says.

I make a point of approaching him further than I need to collect the check, and I breathe through my mouth into his face. "Enjoy the life you've carved out for yourself," I say. "By the way, Reinemarie's husband is on the floor in the viewing room and needs to be cleaned up."

"Get out," Samuel Grillet covers his nose and mouth with his handkerchief. "And don't ever come back here."

I turn once on my way from the room. "She looked more like her dad," I say. "Frankly, I see no other resemblance."

The black Town Car idles outside, and upon opening the back door I find the interior's upholstery lined with sheets of clear plastic. The partition is raised, and I think to yell through it to instruct the driver where to go, but as soon as I close the door the car starts moving. I unfold the check and find Grillet has overpaid. PAY TO THE ORDER OF: Gardiner Blythe—in his meticulous cursive. FOR: Services rendered. I realize I still have X Parke's wires coiled around my shoulder, and I set them on the seat beside me. As the car maunders down the driveway I look back at the mansion, squatting on its hill beneath the crystalline sky, and from a copse of beeches halfway up the slope the sun glints in matching circles of glass, and a small body among the trees, and I look out through the car's back windshield at the faint treads of the car's tires in the powdery snow on the gravel, and I think about how such marks are indicators of something, in their quality of absence are parts of a thing we name to distinguish the thing from itself, or to locate the thing at all . . . or something . . . and I fall asleep and am briefly awakened as the car trundles from the driveway onto a narrow paved road and then quickly fall back to sleep again and dream of X Parke navigating the forests of her own thoughts and wonder how much of it was hers and how much was hers through mine and in my dream there are two columns: X PARKE'S and GARDINER'S, and one is littered with language and the other is bare.

PART IV

The Place of Dense Woods, Great Water

13

The noose remains suspended from the rafter in my kitchen, and the stool remains set beneath it, and so too remains everything else identical to how it was left, though dustier. There's mold in the sink distinctly the same color as my skin, and I discover a plethora of birds' nests arranged on the windowsills and doorframes of the house's interior, but cannot find a point through which the birds may have entered the house, and regardless the nests appear long abandoned. There's no power. I untie the noose and set it along with the coil of wires in the unfinished room at the back of the attic, then collapse into the stiff and oily sheets of my bed, where I sleep late into the night. There was hardly any food in the refrigerator even five years ago, and what little there is—a wedge of cheese, perhaps a lime, something on a plate—has long since shriveled into rockish lumps too dehydrated to constitute rottenness. I find canned meat in the pantry, enough for weeks if I'm abstemious. In the mirror I discover what I already suspected, that my beard and hair are feral, and that my general comportment is of someone mentally ill. I find that after a violent bout of sputtering the shower works fine, and there is a bar of soap that still smells more or less like soap, and I proceed to bathe myself for the first time in five and a half years, then dress in mildewy clothes from the dresser. Afterward, sometime around midnight, I stand on the porch and gape into the void of the nighttime lake, and I hear, from a tree near the house, the sudden solitary shriek of a bird, as if, awakened by a nightmare, it has called out. This stray occurrence, as unremarkable as it may seem, unnerves me in that it pilots my already nervous and fatigued thoughts toward the province of animals' nightmares, this latent crypt of deformed metonyms and decorticated signs—an unpunctuated epilepsy of feverish havoc—an oblique and unmanicured splinter of the literate sum of our human nightmares, which as we all know, can be dreadful enough. I shudder on the porch. What grotesqueries are churned forth by their hindered little brains? What insanities?

In the morning I discover a mulchy pile of mail around the base of the overflowed mailbox at the top of the driveway; only the dozen or so letters inside the box are salvageable. They are bills, mostly, and one residual check (*Grimace, Grimace* appears to have enjoyed a brief resurgence) and at the bottom of the stack a yellowing envelope with my full name, William Gardiner Blythe, hand-printed with a return address for the city. 'Dear William,' the letter reads. 'I am saddened to be writing you after so long without contact in these unfortunate circumstances. I feel the older we get, the more prevalent bad news becomes, and the rarer it is to receive missives that do not proclaim loss. Alas. Marianne Phenix, after a gracefully short battle, has succumbed to her illness. She spoke of you in her final days, before she lost her ability to speak, and asked me to pass along a message, which I am fulfilling herein. She said: "Tell Will not to be too sorry." That is all the context I have for you, unfortunately. I imagine you will grasp the sentiment better than I. Regardless, she went with relative ease, and I imagine was grateful for the repose. Her memorial service will be held at the Church of the Annunciation the last Saturday of this month, on the west side. I know she would want you there, and the rest of us would be delighted—albeit under the circumstances perhaps reserved—to see you after so long. I have been reflecting, in part due to Marianne's death, on the past, specifically the years during which we were all together, pillaging about the city, drawn to the cultivation of mystery and heartbreak and all manner of shenanigans, our lives yawning before us like patches of sprawling meadows, dreaming and dreaming aloud. And like anything so good, its shelf life was short, and while things bittered for all of us—especially you and Marianne, I know—I can say in utter sincerity that I regret nothing. I hope the same for you, and I know, after all these years, that Marianne would as well. She loved you very much, and understood you better than anyone. I will conclude here with a funny story she used to tell about the two of you, and I hope you won't take offense at my sharing it. Apparently this was when you first got together—if I remember correctly you were shacked in that cramped one-bedroom off 8th street that you shared with a family of moody mice—and one night you two argued about something—Marianne could never recall what, but claims it was ultimately banal—and during the argument you threw a book at her, literally, the corner of which nicked her forehead and drew blood, which gave you pause and brought you to your senses, and you reconciled and helped Marianne stem the bleeding, and it turned out the book you'd thrown was a collection of essays by Keirowis Brodisław that Marianne had always struggled to grasp, about which apparently you always gave her a hard time, but that night as you applied a bandage to her head, she held the book in her lap, where a blot of blood marred the corner, and she began to speak about it, about its content, to talk through the more complex conceits, and within hours she was explaining it eloquently and crisply and uncovering meanings within it that had even eluded *you*, and the two of you joked that in being struck by the book its meanings had finally managed to enter her thick skull, and you both found this endlessly amusing, and Marianne continued to find this amusing until the day she died. Anyway, as that is a story you already know, I apologize for the redundancy. I hope to see you at the memorial. Sincerely, Harold Oberman.' Followed by a signature, and a date that is several years past.

Through the small window at the back of my kitchen there's a mess of icy hedge at which upon finishing this letter from my ex-wife's husband I now stare as the hedge sways lazily, and I think about Keirowis Brodisław, whose essays I had nearly forgotten, though who also wrote a number of plays that are more protrusive in my memory, and but now thinking about these essays, which I have not encountered since my twenties, I do recall a sense of the color palate they inspired—this idea of texts being commensurate to certain color palates neither a new thought nor an original one, and something I have long been sensitive to. Brodisław's essays were gray and umber with razor-thin accents of vibrant yellow. One of them, unless I am gravely misremembering, was puce and mustard. The essays' content I cannot recall, having only a vague memory that an aspect of their impenetrability was due to having been poorly translated from the Polish—or else having been written in Polish to begin with. Marianne's problem with them was only in part a result of her own mental laziness and more largely a problem of the essays' bizarre and winding syntax and the at best sporadic and rare sightings of their cruxes. And to further advocate in Marianne's defense, she was not a scholar. The woman enjoyed movies, often campy and profane ones, and only made efforts to digest literary theory for the sake of being closer to me since, by my own youthful pretentions, I refused to meet her at the place of her gaudy cinematic proclivities. There were numerous ways in which Marianne was more willing than I to bridge the gorges between us, namely by appearing at my readings back when they were hosted in windowless bars and boxy twelve-seat theaters, and when I finally sold a book she'd walked around the city with copies in her bag to hand out to anyone she encountered who might be able to positively influence my career. For my own part I can barely remember what Marianne did for work back then—and it's possible, given my incessant blinding self-involvement, that I deliberately avoided memorizing such basic information about her. And so it is no surprise that when she broached the idea of marriage, precisely simultaneous to the outset of the ignition of my career, I at first had balked, and left, and considered her sentimental or impulsive or both for having come so far from out of left-field, when of course the reality was certainly largely on the other side, and I had misread—or rather ignored—the signs, and the more I think about it now the more I appreciate something that has for years been jarringly apparent to me, which is that every way in which I thought other people were misliving their lives was a way that I, through the bleary-eyed goggles of my arrogance and insecurity, was misliving mine.

The lake remains frozen over, and in the afternoon I walk along the shallows. I am struck by the topography of the lakebed, the way the glacial bottom, reddish through the ice, appears in one section like an enormous tongue rolling back into a gathering dark, the tunnel of a throat. I imagine, standing suspended over this gaping mouth, that I am a word, just a syllable, uttered in vain to the sky like trench prayer and fallen on unmoved ears or on nothing at all. This arouses in me an impulse to write—a sensation so foreign by now that at first I mistake it for hunger or exhaustion—and I slide like a droplet of water down a pane of glass across the ice and back to the house, though by the time I arrive the arousal has slackened, and so I sit on the porch and smoke brittle cigarettes from a crumpled pack I'd dug out of my bedside dresser, and I watch a doe standing by the lake's shore as the sky darkens, her fur gray with a membrane of snow, looking off through the serried copse, her eyes gathering what meager light is available to her. Minutely her ears twitch. She appears close enough I could seize her, drag her away into the dark. If I chose to. If I chose I could nestle into her like into a small set of clothes, and speak through her mouth. I could unwrite her from the woods and from the world. I could trade places with her. Her tail swats at the snowflakes suspended in the air like ash from a great fire, and she pads away along the shore. The snow deadens her passage. I could follow her, if I chose.

The snow softens, and it rains for weeks. The lake thaws and the waterline rises, swallowing part of the old dock and the shallow roots of the birch trees on the shore. The unremitting rain inflicts on my sight, even when I am indoors facing a wall or climbing the stairs to the bedroom, the illusion of descending movement, of a falling down of everything. And other, less tenable things begin to happen in my imagination; on the porch, watching rain pit the lake, I imagine, far out in the lake's middle where no one and nothing but the pocks of raindrops had been a moment before, a pair of hands grope out of the water, claw the air, and sink again below the surface. Soon after I imagine a man in the house with me. This man, who by design I never see, is ghoulishly tall and unmoving and stands always just outside the doorframe of whatever room I happen to be in. He does not, as far as I construe, mean me any harm, but his presence, though indemonstrable, dominates the politics of the occupancy of my own house. Distinctly aware of him—looming in the hall or the stairwell—especially at night, I pay careful heed to the weight of my footfalls or the clink of glass against my teeth. This unseen man transforms the nature of my existence in the house. Everything I do is contingent on his position. He is particularly fond of tenanting the stairwell, and so I begin to sleep downstairs, in front of the mantle, entwined with a ratty blanket. I dream of a clammy wall of tumid rocks, deep underground, like the farthest extremity of a cave, replete with blips of water and a musky subterranean smell. I dream of digging upward, and of pawing forth into the forest, and of walking there through creaking and leafless trees, and encountering an abandoned limestone kiln, and rummaging through the debris that surrounds it and finding shards of bone and other imperishable remains, like teeth and, in one case, a set of fingernails. I dream that upon returning home I find that from my porch, where the lake had been, is now a vast, crenulated heath populated by pale, grazing animals. What had been the mountains is now a ridge of enormous blanched teeth, their caps seething in the florid sky. The rampart of pines that had lined the shore—and the occasional lake house huddled among them—is gone; in its place are serried white pillars, thousands of them, a graveyard of uncarved totems. I dream I suffer a heart attack and keel off the porch onto the sopping lawn and sink into the grass like rain. When I wake up I lie on the floor, the blanket knotted around my legs, and I imagine the tall man, looming just around the doorframe, has sewn together, from the dust in the house, a replica of me, and he holds it tight to his unmoving body like an infant.

The rain relents and the days lengthen. My truck's battery is mummified, its tires airless, and something appears to have lived and died in its engine. I walk into town one morning for supplies and find most everything closed save the library and the town's one bar. In the library I discover a mislaid book of Lenape myths. I am reminded of a similar book of Lenape myths that floated around the house in which I grew up. It was an elementary book, each story no longer than a page. As a child I had read that book alongside Aesop and Torqueray and *One Thousand and One Nights* while wearing my pajamas as rain tapped the windowpanes and my mother cried in the other room. Distinctly I am reminded of the smell of that old book, the furfural and musk. I bring this new book to my face and inhale, but it smells different than how I want it to. I leave it where I found it and wander through town to the bar where, despite every instinct, I decide to sit and drink a soda. The bar's patrons—a man about my age with dark and weathered hands, a youngish woman whose efforts to decimate her own beauty with booze and cigarettes and probably some other stronger means have begun to take hold, and the old bartender, whom I recognize though have no name for—are all facing the door when I enter, anticipating my arrival, I think, until I realize they are watching the television mounted to the wall overhead, and I join them, and I sip cola through a straw. Aerial footage of the city, dark and languishing to the horizon, a pall of dinge like the film of a bad eye, and at the northern edge of the tract of park in its middle, suspended from wires or cables that disappear into the augural silver sky, an enormous upside-down pyramid, its point nearly touching the roofs of the buildings lining the park, black and sputtering tufts of fire along its seams, as big as the island's entire northern third. Helicopters flank it; two jets scream past. I order a whiskey, but leave before it arrives; I am, I decide in a brief but sufficient moment of clarity, too tired for combat. I walk back toward my home. To the west: a lock of mountains. I recall spending summers with my father in the shadows of the Wipid Mountains, not far from here. Crags and glens and sallow woods. I used to fire rifles at cans and bottles in the abandoned limestone quarry. Once, my stepbrother had led me and some other boys to a ravine outside of town. Strewn along its nadir: upturned shopping carts, soggy trash bags, a rotted couch. The paludal ground had sucked at our sneakers. There had been a drainpipe at the far end, as wide as a doorway. My stepbrother had made a torch from a stick and a sock steeped in kerosene. The drainpipe had smelled like methane. "Don't make any noise," my stepbrother had hissed. "Or you'll wake her up." The drainpipe had tapered into a dark pocket. Slouched against the metal grate, a terrified expression on her face, a woman, her gray skin indistinguishable from the gray water—indistinguishable from the drainpipe's gray concrete walls. The torch's guttering flame had animated her, so that I'd recoiled from her ceaseless onrush. "Pussy little bitch," my stepbrother had cackled. "She's dead as shit look." He'd thrust the torch into her face and the face had sunk inward and filled with fire and the eyes had bulged outward and contracted it seemed—to me—with panic. One of the other boys had puked in the fetid water. Another had fled toward the daylight. My stepbrother had laughed, twisted the torch. "She's not even real anymore," he'd said. "Just a part of the water." He'd bored holes. The torch's flame had sputtered in the damp. *Soon it will be just one big hole*, I'd thought, I remember now, walking along in the shadow of different mountains.

Back at home I stand on the porch and look out at the lake, dimpled by the wind, and the unceasing lurch of forest beyond. When it grows too dark to see I light candles in the kitchen and attempt to write without conjecture, persuading myself that even a novella will suffice, or a short story. I accomplish neither, failing to form coherent clauses. I dig through a few moldy boxes in the attic for a photo of Marianne that I vaguely recall, but come away with only old notebooks containing a smattering of half-formed sketches—stillborn stories—concerning unintelligible circumstances, and see a great deal of myself where I should see my characters. One such, jotted in the margins of a draft for something else, is reproduced herein, for the sake of disclosure, and unedited:

> It rains for days, sealing Rose Marie in the house. She does not like being indoors for long and grows unnerved—digressing from room to room turning off lights she swears she never turned on; finding doors closed she remembers leaving open and vice versa; standing at windows for long stretches watching the rain gush, unconscionable, with her head tilted slightly and nodding as if at a set of

urgent instructions—and comes to struggle to remember a time before the rain and starts, somewhat facetiously at first but with increasing sincerity, to wonder if she's ever been outside at all. Then very suddenly the rain relents, and the clouds evaporate, and the sun discloses itself and Rose Marie nearly weeps with relief and hurries out into the steeped, lurid landscape to find her garden drowned. Nothing is salvageable save a single gorged tomato dangling close to the ground, which she breaks from its vine and tosses away.

Feeling something akin to homesickness, she sets out to walk the perimeter of the property. The ground sucks at her rain boots and she imagines it laughing, haughtily, with each cumbersome step. The trees, too, that delineate the property lean mockingly inward, as if to get a better look at her discomposure, and the birds that sing from their boughs sing not tunefully but are discordant, tinny, and cruel. As a result Rose Marie is not entirely displeased to find a number of trees fallen here and there, some wrested from their roots, others snapped along their trunks like stalks of celery, and in a wide puddle at the edge of a meadow, a drowned bird, its body swollen, its feathers matted, suspended somewhere between the surface and the sunken grass beneath.

She cuts through a copse at the junction where the property flares west in a grassy corridor the shape of a curled tongue and walks carefully along the exposed ridge of slick limestone running its length. The corridor dilates into a clearing where she finds what at first she mistakes for a pile of branches but which as she approaches she discovers is a clump of overgrown briar—and she realizes she's ventured onto the remote part of the property on which the old house had been years before. She walks around the briar, eying it the way someone might eye unfamiliar food, and she suspects in its own way the briar eyes her back. It looms—twice or three times her height—and she smells a rotten, meaty odor radiating from its interior. Perhaps something has died in it? Drowned like the bird and the garden in the deluge? She wedges a branch inside, feeling for give, but there is nothing except the ligneous snarl of thorns. A damp, cool wind sweeps down the corridor, plating her rain coat and flittering her black hair around the frame of her face, and she thinks she hears the clank of wind chimes from somewhere and looks around and sees only the folds of green and reticulations of brown and white and overhead the generous blue sky spotted with hastening wisps of pale clouds which over the previous days, entombed by the storm, she'd begun to doubt existed at all.

There are marks in the ground, she notices now, nearly like footprints, which lead off around the side of the briar. She follows them, not realizing that she expects to find someone there until she is surprised when there is no one.

The footprints continue around, and when she's made a full rotation she discovers another set of prints alongside the first, and her heart quickens. She stands with her fingers hovering just outside the slits of her raincoat and her elbows cocked away from her body and her stance outspread wider than is natural, convinced she's being toyed with by two trespassers just out of sight on the far side of the briar, snickering silently at her. "I know you're there!" she snaps, and proceeds again around the side of the briar, only to find, once she again makes it the whole way around, a *third* set of prints, these alongside the first two, and she becomes angry, because who do these three think they are, japing a lady on her own property, and she marches around the briar, determined to confront them—and much later, no longer in pursuit of three pranksters but instead, now, being chased by dozens, her lungs churning, scurrying around and around, her shoes unclasping, slipping in the roiled mud, casting terrified glances over her shoulder, always expecting to see the edges of laughing faces breach the briar's rutted perimeter but seeing nothing and this being somehow so much worse and the crinkling of wind chimes or little bells swarming as if the rain has started again except instead of water it is this damned sound falling from the sky and toppling trees and murdering birds and drowning her garden and the appalling rotten smell that reminds her of giving birth in a hospital and of shrill laughter—as the sun disposes itself behind the irregular crowns of the tree line so the air saddens and cools—Rose Marie finally collapses onto her belly in the mud, her shoes unyoked, and cannot get up.

And there are more vignettes involving this same character in equally baffling and only obscurely correlated scenarios, written hastily on scraps of paper, and none for which I grasp a larger context, nor remember writing at all. Some of them proceed as follows:

> Nicole has a rash on her elbows. The ointment Rose Marie applies is smearing all over the kitchen table as Nicole sits drawing a picture of a pale, gangly creature crawling from a fire.
>
> "What is this, baby?" Mel points to the drawing.
>
> "It's smoke," Nicole adds more white.
>
> "Smoke, of course," Mel winks at Rose Marie. Rose Marie gets up to clean the stove.

And another:

> For her birthday, Mel and Rose Marie take Nicole to see Nicole's grandma, Mel's mother, who lives upstate. They drive with the windows half-down and the air is honeyed and the lavish sunlight discloses the world completely as if to vindicate it from charges of connivance. Nicole's hair,

inspired by the wind, crackles around her face and she squints into the front of the car while fishing cheerios from a plastic baggie. "Daddy, is it?" she garbles.

"Is what it, baby?" Mel steers the car with both hands.

But Nicole says nothing else, nor does she speak at all while visiting with Mel's mother, and on the way home—the sun now slouched below the trees and the crepuscular blush of the air perpetually exhaling—Rose Marie blinks into the whirring tree line off the road where she imagines packs of nocturnal animals wearing strange, wide gazes, stepping around the crooks of roots impacted in dirt like molars or fossils, and she imagines them pausing and eying the car as it trundles along, and wonders if these imaginary animals are a sign for her or if the car is a sign for them or if it is possible for them all to be signs for each other.

And one more:

Nicole's little feet writing babbling cursive in the snow and Rose Marie's larger feet undeviating alongside, underscoring the empty message, they stalk the topographical refrain of the land, which clips and swells and hushes them toward a copse beyond which unfolds a narrow corridor of serried pines and the occasional beckoning oak and down the center of which eructs a ridge of icy limestone like the medial sulcus of a tongue. A little while along, the corridor flares into a wide clearing. In its middle looms a hulking mass covered in snow. Through the snow, at sporadic intervals, sprout snarls of thorny vines. Rose Marie approaches it warily, as if she expects it to do something other than exist, transfixed and inanimate. When she is near enough to touch it she pauses, unsettled by the sudden notion that there is someone standing on its far side.

"Bells!" Nicole chirps, and Rose Marie spins, startled at how faraway her daughter's voice is, and is perplexed to see the girl standing many yards back, at the edge of the clearing, when all the while Rose Marie thought she was right beside her.

"Why'd you stop?" Rose Marie traces a shape in the air.

"Bells!" Nicole repeats. Rose Marie turns an ear upward and, in fact, hearing then, faintly, as if from beneath the fallen snow, an atonal clatter, like the shifting of pots and pans on a stove. A clap of wind trespasses Rose Marie's coat and she folds her arms and steps back toward her daughter—but her boot falls on a patch of ice and slips sideways, bowing her knee at an indecent angle and splaying her stance and she goes down onto her ass on the snow. Nicole titters. Rose Marie scooches her legs and tries to rise, but the ice diverts any traction and she flops again, and rolls—she hopes away from this troublesome patch of polished ice—and then tries again, this time keeping her hands planted on the ground and uplifting her rear and setting one foot at a time, carefully, on the snow and manages to erect herself into a sort of precarious yoga pose at which point she lifts one hand from the ground and a moment later her feet slide backward and she thumps onto her belly. Nicole meanwhile, imagining the rubbery slapstick noises from the cartoons on TV—the boings and zips and stammers—laughs and claps and hops with delight at her silly mommy. Rose Marie curses into the snow, her breath outpouring like exhaust, and tries, again, to stand, and again flops and topples and rolls and tries again and again and pauses, inhales, exhales, tries again and thinks she's got it this time and carefully, shakily, rises onto her legs, her arms outspread, waits for herself to still, takes a step, and slides out, landing nastily on her hip. Nicole cackles, her eyes spotted with tears, unconscionable, and prays it will never stop.

These strange snapshots of a half-realized family doing little for me by way of inspiring involution, and because I am unable to be productive now in the way I want, feel neither inquisitive nor focused nor aroused nor enjoy appetite nor even particularly an urge to drink, I am, by the end of spring, back in the same throes of anhedonia that inspired me to drastic action five-and-a-half years ago. Everyday I find another bird's nest I'd failed to notice, and dispose of it. I think of Marianne, her unbearable good humor, her exaggerated self-appraisal as a talented chef, the knuckly points of her knees prodding me on our sidewalk-salvaged sofa while I beat and combed and flayed at my first novel—and none of this, despite my intellectual appreciation of its sentimentality, stirs in me anything but vague pride at the tenacity of my old mind's recall. I remember the first time I'd met her parents. They lived west of the city's suburbs, a rural region to which I'd struggled to reconcile Marianne's quintessential hipsterisms and practiced—if somewhat challenged—sophistication. Her parents did little to mitigate this discrepancy; they were quaint in the plainest sense, all handshakes and eye contact with flags embroidered on the decorative pillows in their living room. There was no alcohol in the house, so I'd gone to the bathroom to ingest a haphazardly curated cocktail of pills, the effects of which were impossible to predict, and which in that particular case had made me angry, and I'd picked a fight with Marianne at the dinner table and had called her names and had generally mocked her in front of her parents, both of whom had eaten their salads very tactfully and nodded as if they had agreed with my vicious and unfounded indictments of their daughter, who, for her part, was so used to my attacks by then that she had responded merely with her faint smile and a sequence of diplomatic shrugs, and after dinner—of which I remember eating none—Marianne's parents had seen us off warmly, her father taking an extra moment to let me know that if I ever needed anything, he was there, and on the way back to the city Marianne had thanked me profusely for agreeing to go with her, that she knew these things were not easy for me. And I had convinced her to go drinking at a few bars near our apartment, and don't remember the rest of the night. But I do remember coming to the following morning on the sofa, still drunk and consumed by the vague, guttering resonance of a terrible rage. I'd found Marianne in the bedroom, snarled in the sheets, and had spent the morning rearranging sentences around the chapter I was lost in, and at noon Marianne had appeared in the doorway, her mouth affixed in that soft smile. I think she had asked if I'd wanted whiskey in my coffee. There had been another time, I remember now while gazing at the steep pine-needle-strewn lawn from the porch and the dilapidated shed nestled in trees by the water and the stalwart boulders along the shallows like rows of fingers and the bracing elegance of the wind-dimpled water and jungly shore of pines foregrounding the mountain range, when Marianne and I'd gone to one of my early readings at a bookstore uptown which only a sprinkling of friends and industry gophers had attended, and after the reading I'd been approached by a young woman, an editor at some since defunct literary magazine, who had solicited a piece and invited me for a drink, and Marianne, who had been standing right there smiling, had started to leave with us, trailing behind, and outside the bookstore I'd stopped and taken her aside and told her I'd see her at home, that this was business better conducted on my own, and her smile had never wavered and she'd merely raked her fingernails down my forearm and waved goodnight to the gorgeous editor and had headed off down the sidewalk alone and I think it was days before I'd made it home again, and when I did Marianne had been glad to see me, and had taken my clothes to the laundromat while I showered and slept, and she'd made dinner I think, and told me she was pregnant, to which I'd told her to get an abortion. I was much older than her, and never wanted children. She'd nodded and smiled with wet eyes, and said "No." It was the only time I'd ever heard her use the word, and we'd fought, and I'd left. Though of course I'd returned. I cannot remember what my self-righteous rationalizations must have been at the time, but understanding now that I needed her, needed from her her unwavering decency and the promise of something bigger than myself. Though with how things ended up I should have just spared her the additional thirteen years of abuse, and the culminating trauma of our loss, and stayed away or killed myself.

Our daughter looked so much like her, but with my mind. Fiercely astute. I will not dare to write her name. Her upbringing ladened Marianne with a gravity of which I hadn't known she was capable, grayed her hair and hardened the smile off her face. There were good years then. My books sold, and I drank somewhat less. Our daughter was a wonder and an inspiration, her thoughts straddling an envious codistinction between random whimsy and stark analysis. She was obsessed with spaces behind objects, the spaces she couldn't see. I would catch her peaking around the back of the sofa, or the edge of my desk, furtively, as if were she quiet enough she could catch whatever strange laws governed this fantastical preoccupation in the act. Marianne of course was in love with her too, but about some other characteristic, some other charm that I couldn't see. I do ask myself now if this particular way in which I was anamoured with our daughter was not selfish, was not for the pure idiom of youthful imagination and the writer's frantic and futile journey to reclaim that state. Was I using her to espy a part of myself into which there was no other view? Was the way in which Marianne loved her cleaner than my way? But life was easy then—or so it seems from here—and we were happy. We even considered having another child, but never got around to it. And the one was enough. She was all the ways in which Marianne and I were not each other; she softened me and hardened her mother. She was beautiful in her own way, as a baby and as a child, and was becoming a beautiful teenager. She would be somewhere in college now, starting her own life. I cannot believe how much I have aged in so short a time. They say having children keeps you young. They don't say anything about losing a child.

It was Marianne who left the last time. Abruptly, or so it felt. I was too steeped in whiskey to know any longer the difference between abrupt and well-earned. I remember her in the doorway to my study, her coat half-buttoned, nothing soft about her face and nothing decent about anything. "I'm going to the city," she'd said.

Our daughter had been gone for eleven months. "I know it was that boy," I'd said against the rim of my glass. "He's sick. That lawyer of his is pulling strings to conceal his charges, but I've heard. I've heard what people say about him. Jerking off in front of those girls. Those threats he sent to the school. Remember she said, that one day, that someone had followed her home? It was him. I know it was him. And he took her. And he did. . . . He did it. . . ."

"I'm going to the city," Marianne had repeated, and then the doorway was empty, and the house was empty, and soon after my glass was empty, and then full again, and then I was lost in spates of night and acrid sunlight, and a maddening maze of not knowing. It was that boy. Or one of her teachers. It was someone. I sent scores of supplication to the police, meticulous diagrams, winding explanations, even dual columns into which I logged the reasons it was the boy or one of her teachers. They were kind and engaged at first. I know they spoke to the boy. I know they spent time at the school. But soon they grew tired of me, and their focus drifted to more closable cases. I was left even further alone than I was without Marianne and my daughter. I could write nothing but explication as to the boy's guilt—or the guilt of one of her teachers. I obsessed flagrantly over what her life might be, over what she might be thinking were she here, her staggering imagination and precise analytics, learning to navigate the pathless tracts of life. Her grace and wit. The friends she might have made, and the lovers. The preternatural curiosities entrenched in the very banal. The way she thought about the parts of things she couldn't see. Her hair just like Marianne's. And the whiskey ran on and on and the house shrank around me, entombed me until I was stuck in it like inside a set of child's clothes, each limb lodged in a separate room. It was there that I began to feel the panic and the anger and the interminable sadness recede like tide from a carcassy-smelling littoral, and in this release and its sinister serenity I found I felt nothing anymore at all, and that I had mourned her sufficiently, and that now, after all this time, she was finally actually gone. That is when I fashioned the noose, and secured it to the rafter in the kitchen. I didn't even bother to write a note, since as a novelist I have in essence been writing my suicide note my whole life, and besides I could produce nothing of value and nothing that no one else could not say about me. It was a just and well-earned and wholly unabrupt end for me. I knew better then as I know still now that I would join no one where I was going. It occurred to me that this gesture would be the truest art I had made since my youth. Though like other opportunities to make true art that one too was interrupted by what I now understand was a wasteful and pointless idea. It was a desperate and cowardly effort to reclaim something that was irrevocably gone from me. I am embarrassed by what it must say about the disposition of my character; for one who has written with purported authority about the inseparability of life and loss, and about the meaninglessness of death, I raged insolently against my own loss, and took too earnestly to the finality of my own death.

Thinking through all this I am reminded why I write, what I aim to excavate and vanquish when I write, how I seek to both uncoil and complicate the sharp ligatures of my past, and to name the parts of my present. It is in worship of the thing itself. To affirm the existence of the thing through a worship of its parts. Though worship, perhaps, implies futility: Worship is an attempt to reconcile the parts with the thing. It is the action of scrutinizing parts in search of some aspect of the thing itself, but founders, as a preoccupation with parts under the illation that through those parts some quality of the thing can be realized. It cannot. A scrutinizing of parts can only determine aspects of the parts themselves. The thing has no aspect. The thing cannot be addressed outside of naming the postulation of its entirety. Which is perhaps a half-way decent argument against worship, or theism generally, though I have neither the energy nor interest in pursuing such litigation here. My intent is not to justify one operation over another. Susan Sontag wrote that 'the world (all there is) cannot, ultimately, be justified. Justification is an operation of the mind which can be performed only when we consider one part of the world in relation to another—not when we encounter all there is.' To put it plainly: to search for the truth of the entirety in any capricious section of it is akin to amputating your teenager's finger and then paying to put the finger through college. Which is a crass analogy. But I am done with tact.

But the writing itself—despite any digressions to the contrary—is a pursuit of self-actualization. I write because when I do not, I feel simultaneously remote and indistinguishable from the world. I feel futile. So to actualize myself. And yet even when I *do* write I am often so preoccupied with the trappings of style for the sake of evacuating myself that I lose sight of the divine pleasure of a good story simply told. And I avoid myself at any cost. So I am damned either way, and the entire enterprise has failed me.

This is why I am compelled again, after being interrupted five and a half years ago, to retrieve the noose from the attic, and clear the ill-derived version of myself that lurches soulless without distinction from the otherwise perfect world. The flindering green door separating the finished attic from the unfinished attic sticks on its frame and I shoulder it open. I find the noose fraying and frangible and fear it won't hold, so I fashion a second noose from a coil of wires I find beside it, and fasten that from the rafter in the kitchen. I take a moment to stand at a notepad on the kitchen table, and I dangle a pen over it as if ink might drip out and spell a code to stave my intent. A word, or a gash of words. A glassy sentence, an uncouth paragraph, a page or two of incoherence. A poem disguised as a story missing its middle. Or a novel that unfurls like a forest fire. A question mark. A comma. A spiral. A line. But the notepad is blank, and the pen is dry. And I kick at the stool until it's under the wires, and standing there I notice another bird's nest, this atop the refrigerator, and from the nest's rim a pair of black eyes quaver, following the arc of the wires as I wrestle them under my beard and onto my throat. Not bird's eyes. If Marianne and I had had a second child, then I could have mourned the loss of our first, and lived for that grief. But I have become the sallow graveyard of a man. Or if I'd been blessed to be born anything but a writer . . . I miss everyone terribly. I never owned a dog. I should have read more.

There's a scratching sound now from the front of the house, and a distant voice. I stand with my socked toes curled around the edge of the stool, waiting for the sound to recede into my imagination, but it does not. Warily I free myself and alight, and skulk through the creaking house to the front door. Not scratching, but meager knocking, and a small voice calling, "Hello? Mister Blythe? Hello?" There are scant western-facing windows here, and the house darkens in the afternoon, and I feel for the door's knob and turn it, and there's a girl there on my front porch, a nest of auburn hair and thick glasses and a stuffed backpack, one nubby hand still raised to strike the door, the other kneading something made of paper or glass that I cannot identify, and her feet step and shuffle in place as if she's on the verge of urinating, and she blinks and frowns at me and says, "I need your help."

"Who are you?"

"It's me," the girl fidgets. "Hobbes Nicole X Parke's sister."

There's a batting of wings from upstairs. "Right," I say. "Of course."

"I need your help can I come in?"

"How did you find me?"

"Mister Grillet keeps a log of all the trips his car makes so I checked the log and there were a few addresses there and I wasn't sure which one was yours but then I remembered when you drove away I saw the car turn north from the driveway and this address was the only one north of ours so I came here now can I come in?"

I make her wait while I reset the stool at the table and toss the wires over the rafter so it appears as innocuous as electrical maintenance, then wave her inside. She scurries past me and drops her backpack to the floor and then paces just inside the hallway, blinking around. She is small for her age, I assume, and largely prepubescent.

"What is it you want?" I fold myself in a chair near the door.

"X Parke's missing and I know where they took her but I can't go on my own because I don't know what to do when I get there and also nobody remembers her except me but I think you do too because you know the people who took her and also I don't want to point fingers but it's kind of your fault that she's gone not that you meant to or anything but if it wasn't for you then she wouldn't be gone probably and anyway I think you owe it to her to help rescue her because the people who took her are evil I think or maybe there's no such thing as evil but they definitely don't have X Parke's best interests in mind and we need to get her back because she's my sister and she'd do the same for me and there's a lot of bird's nests in here did you know that bird's nests actually have multiple rooms in them like a house and to the bird these rooms are all distinct and serve their own distinct purposes but to people it all just looks like one big room?"

"And where is your sister, exactly?"

"In the city," Hobbes Nicole outspreads her arms and upturns her hands in such a way that reminds me of everything. "Don't you read the news?"

"No, I don't."

"You remind me of my grandpa he used to also not read the news and you kind of look like him also but uglier no offense it's not your fault but my grandpa was really handsome he lived through the Fire and all of it and he used to take me to the museum to see the whale you know the one with the big eye in the dark just kind of floating there and I used to be able to see myself in the whale's eye and I looked like myself except small and darker and kind of round because the eye was round and my grandpa told me that whales have the biggest brains of any animal and that you can actually get electrocuted and die from the synapses of whales' brains because they're so powerful and he *also* told me that whales have hands inside their fins which to be honest doesn't sound true to me but anyway that's where X Parke is she's in the city with the man with the ponytail and the boy who was with him who's maybe his son I think but I don't know for sure is he his son?"

"No."

"Well whoever he is he's keeping X Parke there against her will and I have to go save her and you need to come with me."

A rush of thoughts accost me here: the echoing frozen woods thawing and thickening and surging open; streams chattering down cliffs and emptying into gullies; meadows unfurling their dissonant emptinesses; footprints; unimaginable dangers to be confronted and thought through and overcome; a rescue mission; friends and enemies; a task at hand; sustenance for the language starved and language for the parameters of parts yet undescribed; campfires; crags and boulders and distant mountains and steep ravines through which pale creatures gangle; a knife glinting at the shore of a lake as deep and wide as the sky; trees recoiling from the agonized crook of a tower with no doors or windows; the weedy trellises of train tracks and rotted smokestacks and fire; the demented and disillusioned; a throne and a boy; a girl with no past, no future, who never knew me; fury; futility and retreat; another arduous journey home, empty handed; the panicked and outrageous mind of a child sorting the forest through its gaze; a glass house on a hill; wind and bells; a thuck of briar; pathless; a place of dense woods and great water; and company, a voice other than my own; something new; something else. The possibilities. The punctuationless grammar of the forest. The sky. The wet earth. "Maybe tomorrow," I say, rising from the chair and going to stand on the porch.

Later I give Hobbes Nicole my bedroom and take my place on the floor by the mantle. There was nothing to eat in the house and in the morning I will have to walk into town for food—regardless of whether or not I accompany her any further. I do not know yet. Maybe tomorrow I will draw two columns, and weigh my options.

Around midnight the stairs moan, and I pretend to be asleep as Hobbes Nicole steps over me and outside. I watch her in the moonlight, leaning over the porch's railing and scanning the back lawn. She sees the shed down near the water and climbs from the porch and starts toward it. I wonder what she imagines it contains. As she goes, the night breathes, the whole thing secreting its palate, dark red and forest green and thick panes of white, the occasional gash of vibrant neon, and halfway to the dark shape of the shed she pauses, and starts to turn around, but something drives her on, her arms angled away from her body, and I turn and secure the blankets over my face, not needing to watch any further, knowing already what happens next.

MAX HALPER is the author of the novella, *Lamella*, and numerous short fictions. He lives in Upstate New York.